# Exclusively
## Chloe

## J. A. Yang

**speak**
An Imprint of Penguin Group (USA) Inc.

SPEAK

Published by the Penguin Group

Penguin Group (USA) Inc., 345 Hudson Street, New York, New York 10014, U.S.A.

Penguin Group (Canada), 90 Eglinton Avenue East, Suite 700, Toronto, Ontario, Canada M4P 2Y3
(a division of Pearson Penguin Canada Inc.)

Penguin Books Ltd, 80 Strand, London WC2R 0RL, England

Penguin Ireland, 25 St Stephen's Green, Dublin 2, Ireland (a division of Penguin Books Ltd)

Penguin Group (Australia), 250 Camberwell Road, Camberwell, Victoria 3124, Australia
(a division of Pearson Australia Group Pty Ltd)

Penguin Books India Pvt Ltd, 11 Community Centre,
Panchsheel Park, New Delhi - 110 017, India

Penguin Group (NZ), 67 Apollo Drive, Rosedale, North Shore 0632, New Zealand
(a division of Pearson New Zealand Ltd.)

Penguin Books (South Africa) (Pty) Ltd, 24 Sturdee Avenue,
Rosebank, Johannesburg 2196, South Africa

Registered Offices: Penguin Books Ltd, 80 Strand, London WC2R 0RL, England

First published in the United States of America by Speak,
an imprint of Penguin Group (USA) Inc., 2009

1 3 5 7 9 10 8 6 4 2

Copyright © J. A. Yang, 2009
All rights reserved

LIBRARY OF CONGRESS CATALOGING-IN-PUBLICATION DATA

Yang, J. A.
Exclusively Chloe / by J.A. Yang.
p. cm.
Summary: In the public eye since she was adopted as a baby
from China by her Hollywood celebrity parents, sixteen-year-old Chloe-Grace,
longing for a "normal" life, undergoes a transformation with the help of her mother's stylist
and finds not only the life she wanted but an important key to her past.
ISBN 978-0-14-241226-8 (pbk.)
[1. Fame—Fiction. 2. Identity—Fiction. 3. Intercountry adoption—Fiction. 4. Adoption—Fiction.
5. Family problems—Fiction. 6. Interpersonal relations—Fiction.] I. Title.
PZ7.Y19335Ex 2009    [Fic]—dc22    2008041032

Speak ISBN 978-0-14-241226-8
Printed in the United States of America

PUBLISHER'S NOTE

This is a work of fiction. Names, characters, places, and incidents are either the product of
the author's imagination or used fictitiously, and any resemblance to actual persons,
living or dead, businesses, companies, events, or locales is entirely coincidental.

To Lilly,
My agent, my life

## ACKNOWLEDGMENTS

My utmost thanks to Chloe's fairy godmothers: Stephanie Von Borstel and Lilly Ghahremani at Full Circle Literary, and Karen Chaplin and Grace Lee at Penguin. Without your patience and amazing support, CG might have never entered the spotlight.

# Chapter
## 1

"Chloe-Grace!"

I stopped walking and automatically turned around. It's a reflex from a lifetime spent on red carpets. Even when surprised, I've been conditioned to turn around glamorously, which means with slight hesitation and a tilt of the head before throwing my face up and out.

I smoothed my long black hair out of my face and smiled.

"Ohmigod, it IS you. I knew it!" My smile quickly faded as I saw two middle-aged women staring at me. Crap. I'd been spotted.

Then again, that might kind of be my fault. Tourists in the know understand that when searching for stars, weekday afternoons are the time to find them hanging around Beverly Hills. Weekends are for attention whores; weekdays are when the *real* celebrities get their shopping and errands done. I'd figured I would be safe.

Apparently not.

I normally wouldn't be caught dead on Rodeo Drive without a partner in crime, but this wasn't exactly a preplanned excursion. Mrs. Delphy's pretest geometry review was shaping up to be intensely boring, so I'd taken off when I had the chance. Besides, I was doing great in geometry already. A-students deserve to ditch once in a while, too, right?

The two started walking toward me, one pulling out her camera, the other searching her purse, no doubt for a pen and paper for my autograph. From fifty feet away, I'd say they were from Iowa—nobody willingly subjected themselves to matching IOWA . . . WE'RE SO CORNY T-shirts unless they were actually from Iowa—but I wasn't sticking around to find out.

"Chloe-Grace! Chloe—" I turned and started speed walking away. I ducked and covered into the closest store, which turned out to be Cartier, practically my home away from home.

I was still looking over my shoulder as I pulled the door closed and ran straight into someone.

"*Mon dieu*, Chloe-Grace!" Jean-Paul exclaimed. My favorite retail therapist was 5 feet 5½ inches tall, just like me, but proportioned like the Eiffel Tower, hefty side down, and barely moved by my small frame.

"Why didn't you call us beforehand, Chloe? I could have prepared something special for you to look at."

"JP, don't worry about it. I'm just dropping by. Would you mind locking that door, though? I've got some celeb stalkers on my tail."

"*Oui, oui*, of course, of course." Jean-Paul regained his

composure and reached around me to flick the lock closed. "They're everywhere, huh?" He took my bag and reached for my hand, leading me toward the back of the store. I loved Jean-Paul because he had this knack for finding the most adorable little accessories. That, plus we felt bonded cosmically by our life situation: We are both of Asian descent but were adopted by non-Asian parents. His parents are French, mine are famous: an Oscar Award–winning mom and a rock star dad.

The superfans had just arrived at the entrance, and I watched them peering in after giving the door a few unsuccessful shakes.

"So, what will we be looking at today?" Jean-Paul said, giving an amused glance out the double doors. "Another diamond? Some pearl earrings perhaps?"

I turned back to Jean-Paul and smiled. With the fans safely locked outside, I was given a chance to breathe and relax. And nothing relaxes a girl like Cartier display racks and the sudden need for a new bracelet to complete an outfit.

"Hmm. I think I'm looking for something with green in it."

"Well, let's make those dreams a reality, shall we?" I happily followed Jean-Paul to one of the display racks.

A half hour and one emerald and platinum charm bracelet later, it was still too early for Austin, my ex-boyfriend and the former future Mr. Chloe-Grace, to pick me up. As a senior, he was allowed to leave campus during his free periods, and he'd dropped me off earlier.

With more shopping ahead of me, I needed to refuel and

walked over to Great Eats Market to feed my addiction: gummy penguins—have you had them? They're peach flavored and to die for, but impossible to find except at the Beverly Hills location.

My smile disappeared after just five minutes inside, however, as I already regretted not bringing my mom's floppy hat and big sunglasses—her "housewife outfit" as she called it. While the Beverly Hills's Great Eats crowd was too cool to call me out, they weren't too cool to stare. It seemed a bit strange, actually. Spotting a celebrity here was almost as regular an occurrence as the daily specials. As I wandered to the candy bins at the back of the store, I started to feel self-conscious. What? Did my outfit not match or something?

Ignoring everyone, I took two scoops of gummies with me to the register, after taste testing a few chocolates along the way, of course. As I dug through my Versace clutch for some money, I looked up and saw it: the cover of *Celeb Weekly*.

My mom's face was staring back at me, the picture taken from when she headlined the list of Most Beautiful Celebrities Ever: 10th Anniversary Edition. Big black letters next to her picture read "Divorced!" Inset was a smaller picture of my dad kissing Caroline Treasure, a woman whose face wouldn't rank on any most beautiful list—ever. In bold letters next to this stomach-churning picture? "Cheater!" Suddenly the awkward staring made sense, and I immediately lost my desire for gummies. I grabbed the magazine off the rack, threw down some money, and ran out, exit stage right.

Huddled on a bench, I read the entire article—twice. My dad

used to tease my mom, saying that someday her beauty would fade and then he'd run off with a younger woman. Turns out my dad was a prophet, as well as the front man of Two Ounces of Gold—two and a half hit wonders from 1999. I guess he did get his younger woman, but got caught doing it. I reminded myself that this was a tabloid; but even still, some of those stories did have some truth to them. I had to find out what was going on. I had to get home.

I fished through my bag for my cell phone.

"Austin! I need you to come get me, like, right now," I said when he picked up.

"Chloe, what's the big rush?" He sounded out of breath.

"I need to get home—immediately. It's an emergency." I didn't mean to sound dramatic, but I couldn't take this. I was reeling from the article.

"No way. I can't," he said, clearly annoyed. "We're not done with practice yet. I thought I said after five. You told me that would be fine. Can't you just wait or call Rachelle?"

"I can't wait, okay? And Rachelle is still in class. Please, you have to come get me. My life is falling apart." My voice cracked, and I felt tears begin to well up in my eyes.

"Jeez, if you're going to cry about it. Hang on a second." I could hear him muffle his speaker. "Fine, I'll be right there."

"I'm across the street from Great Eats Market. Just hur—"

*Click.* I can't believe he hung up on me at a time like this. I put my phone back in my purse and started pacing back and forth, trying to walk off my growing anxiety.

What were the actual chances that my parents were really getting divorced? I wish I could say that there was no way it could possibly happen. The truth was, I wasn't really sure. And this was *Celeb Weekly*—a tabloid, yes, but one that was slightly reputable. If it was *Fame* or *Spotlight*, it would have been easier to dismiss.

The thing was, I didn't really know what my parents were up to anymore. When I was younger, it was so different. My dad stayed at home and took care of me. And even though my mom was always busy filming on location, she tried to be around as much as she could. But last year all this changed when my dad went back into the studio to make another album (don't call it a comeback album; he hates that). I guess I'd heard that he'd been out at clubs and stuff, but that was just for publicity reasons, right?

My thoughts were interrupted as Austin's Audi S4 pulled up to the sidewalk. If he still cared about me at all, he sure didn't act like it. Engine revving and with barely a glance in my direction, he brusquely popped open the passenger door. "You gotta stop doing this. You can't just cry every time you want something."

I got into the car; but before I could even show him the magazine and explain myself, he started talking again, this time with a lot more volume than necessary. "You know I'm going to get in trouble for this, right? Coach might not let me start because of leaving practice."

"Wait a second!" I said defensively. "You missed an entire basketball practice last week to hang out with Josie Wails—the most notoriously easy girl at school, I might add—and now you're upset because you already used a get-out-of-jail card on her?"

Austin whipped his head around toward me, and his pale blue eyes turned icy. "Look, I can do whatever I want, when I want. You don't get to be jealous anymore. You broke up with me, remember?"

He had a good point; but I wasn't about to back down, especially when I could replace rationality with volume. "I broke up with you because you said you were too busy to hang out with me! I asked you to make more time for us, and you didn't." By this time, my usual scratchy voice had edged into shrieking harpy territory.

A little backstory on our relationship: Austin and I'd been together for a year and a half; we were the Newton "it" couple. My mom is the famous actress; his dad is the famous agent. But sometime during our relationship, I'd wondered if Austin had been told by his dad to date me just because of my mom. Stupid, I know. But the few times I'd met his dad, he'd way too casually asked me if my mom was looking for new representation. I guess he was looking for new clients, particularly one of the most sought-after stars in Hollywood.

That, combined with the fact that Austin always wanted to hang out with his friends, go to parties, or do things that seemed to involve groups of people, started to get on my nerves. Yes, he was fun and made me laugh, and we were kind of this super-couple that everyone was always talking about and admiring, but that was about the extent of it. So I decided to dump him. That was three weeks ago.

Austin rolled his eyes. "Whatever, just tell me where you need to go."

"Just take me home," I said, suddenly remembering why I'd asked him to pick me up in the first place. I didn't want to keep arguing with him; it would go nowhere, as usual.

For the rest of the fifteen-minute ride home, we sat in stony silence; but by the time he pulled through the gates of my house, I had cooled off and was even a tiny bit apologetic.

"Austin, look, I'm sorry for making you pick me up and—"

"Whatever," he said, rudely interrupting. "I have to go. I told Coach I'd be right back."

I looked at him as he stared straight ahead. "Fine," I mumbled, and opened the door and ran out without a wave, thank-you, or good-bye. Good riddance.

As he sped away, I walked up the steps through our arched doorway and pushed open the twenty-foot-high wooden doors. The tabloid article came crashing back to mind, and I dropped my bags and headed through our downstairs "show kitchen" toward my mom's preferred midafternoon lounging place—the pool and back patio. But as I stepped outside, all I saw was the pool attendant.

"Mom, where are you?" I shouted, almost frantically. I went back into the house toward the east wing and headed upstairs, where I heard noises in the room across from the staircase.

"Mom, is that you?" I poked my head in and found only Gracela, our head maid, busy cleaning the contents of the trophy room.

"Hey, Gracela? Do you know where my mom is?"

She turned around and smiled. "Chloe-Grace. Sorry, I'm not

sure where your mom went," Gracela said, as she returned to gently dusting her way around my mom's Golden Globes, MTV Movie Awards, and Oscar for Best Actress in a Supporting Role—positioned prominently in the center of the room on a ceremonial dais. "She left a few hours ago."

"Oh, okay. Thanks," I replied, as she gathered her supplies and left the room.

I took a minute and stepped in and looked around. I hardly ever came into this room. It is dominated by a huge replica of a platinum record, five feet tall and equally wide. My dad received only two gold records in his career; but his fuzzy math said that two gold records equaled one platinum one, so he had the giant silver platter made. The two certified gold records sit framed to the right, dwarfed by their shinier offspring. When you walk in, you can't help but stare at the "platinum" record, which is exactly its purpose. It also doubles nicely as a mirror.

The rest of the room was filled with framed magazine covers (mostly my mom's), various other awards and trophies, souvenirs from charity balls, autographs from famous friends, and in the left corner, an area dedicated entirely to me.

I went over to take a look at my favorite picture—the one of me, eleven months old, coming off a Singapore Airlines plane with my parents. Actually, you can barely see anything except my head poking out of a bundle of blankets. My parents are wearing ill-fitting Chinese ceremonial clothing and look a little silly in the picture—if that was even possible for two such photogenic people. My mom's traditional Chinese *qipao* dress was clearly way too short for her, although that could have been by design. My dad was wearing one of those broad-rimmed bamboo hats tilted off his head at a ridiculous angle, probably so as not to mess up his spiky black hair. They both looked as if they were playing dress up or were in costume for a movie.

This particular photo was on the cover of *People*. Being the first major celebrity adoption didn't exactly make me anonymous. Years ago, during an interview about her upcoming wedding plans, my mom had declared that she didn't want to have children; but then, a few months after that interview, right after my parents' honeymoon, she brought me back with her after a highly publicized humanitarian trip to China.

Of course, once my parents adopted me, an entire avalanche of celebrity adoptions ensued. The celebrity stork logged some serious first-class mileage. Tibet, Malawi, Cambodia, Ethiopia, Yemen—every developing country was soon represented in the loving and eager arms of Hollywood's brightest young stars.

My mom loved it. She was setting trends by declaring that adoption was the hip new way to start a family for a celebrity couple. And the public ate it up.

Pictures of me were immediately plastered all over every glossy. I was proclaimed by every news network to be the cutest Chinese export since Xiao Mei the panda. Entertainment shows polled the public about whether or not I should maintain my given name, Shao-Chi, or be given an Americanized one. The exclusive pictorial rights to my first three birthday parties were sold for hundreds of thousands of dollars. A year ago, *Starz Magazine* did a two-page foldout of all of my school pictures. At my insistence, that issue's not framed in the trophy room. I may have been gloriously cute as a baby, especially dressed in every trendy outfit my mom could find; but I wasn't, as some people (obviously) pointed out, the actual genetic offspring of two perfectly proportioned celebrities. Bad enough I wasn't statuesque like my mom or the owner of chiseled cheekbones like my dad. My face was a bit too oval, my nose a tad too flat, and my eyes a little too narrow to be considered classically beautiful. But I also had to put up with constant speculation about what a birth baby from them would look like.

I sighed and took one last look at my wall of photos. Everything seemed so much simpler in that one photo. Before all the Hollywood craziness. I shook my head and left the trophy room. Without knowing where my mom was, or when she was likely to return, I decided I should take my mind off this divorce rumor—yes, I was calling it a rumor—by calling Rachelle. My best friend and partner in retail crime would know how to make me feel better.

I grabbed my cell from my bag and headed to my room (decorated "Chinese style," of course, complete with plush Oriental rugs, traditional Chinese paintings, and even Chinese characters for *eternal love* in big letters over my bed. Once I grew old enough to realize how tacky everything was, I put up my own posters, so at one point Justin Timberlake was heroically posed among the picturesque valleys and rivers of China).

Sitting on my bed, I dialed Rachelle's number, but before I could press the last digit, my door opened.

"Chloe, what are you doing home?"

"Mom!" She looked worn-out but still beautiful, standing poised and erect in her satin pearl empire dress. Bell sleeves dangled over unseen hands. Her pale blue eyes were misty with a chance of rain, and her auburn hair seemed to need some serious antistatic cling action. "You're home!" I clicked my cell closed and walked over to her, and we did our requisite air-kisses. Not that my mom is one of those celebrities who is fake and shallow or anything. This was just our signature way of greeting each other. "What's this about Caroline Treasure?" I blurted out before she could even say anything.

Her right eyebrow raised a bit, not quite her famous right-eyebrow raise from her most popular romantic comedy to date, *The Beginning of the End*, but close to that.

Taking a deep breath, she said, "You heard the news too?"

"So, it's true? Dad cheated on you with Caroline Treasure?"

My mom's entire body seemed to sag just a little as she walked over and sat on the edge of my bed. "Darling, please, your father and I have been having problems," she continued, her voice sounding apologetic. "We're both so busy all the time, and it's just been really hard lately."

Slipping out of her high heels and digging her toes into the carpet, my mom continued. "We both know your dad's been trying hard to make a comeback. It's unfair to saddle him with pressures from home while he's busy carving out another career."

I'd kind of been hoping my mom would refute the story—get

instantaneously angry or something—not sound as if she already knew about it, or accepted it.

"Your father hasn't exactly been faithful; whether that's with Caroline or not, I don't know."

"Mom, Dad shouldn't be cheating on you, no matter how busy you guys are."

"I know, which is why I filed for the divorce. I was going to tell you about it, but I was hoping to have your dad here so we could break the news to you together. I'm sorry you had to find out this way."

I sucked in a breath. So there it was. My parents, who had adopted me as a symbol of their undying love, were now divorcing. Confirmed and for real. Where did that leave me?

"It's the right thing to do," she went on. "We can't make your father happy, and he can't make us happy, so there's no need for him to continually disrespect us by showing up around town with the trashy Caroline Treasures of the world. It's okay, Chloe. Life goes on; we live longer; we get stronger."

I think that last line was part of her monologue from her romantic drama *Until the Dawn*. Whatever it was, it worked; and she collapsed onto her knees, crying. I on the other hand was left wondering about the "we" in "We can't make your father happy."

# Chapter
## 2

The next morning I woke up hoping yesterday had just been a dream. But as I turned over to shut off my alarm, I caught a glimpse of the tabloid magazine on my nightstand, and I couldn't help collapsing back into bed. Reaching out, I grabbed my phone. No messages, no texts. Nothing.

I was surprised that Rachelle hadn't called or texted me. She was always on top of this type of news. Letting my head sink into the pillow, I felt absolutely drained and defeated before the day had even started. I took a deep breath. There was no choice but to just face reality. It was a school day, and I had to deal with the masses.

My drive to school was less than thirty minutes. When I entered through the gates, I sighed, preparing myself for the gossip I was about to endure. Newton School for the Gifted was very exclusive and superprivileged—unofficially dubbed Celebrity High. It was flush with a student population whose last names competed with the Hollywood Walk of Fame for prestige. I wasn't the only famous kid here, not by a long shot. But while there were plenty of star brats on campus, not many of them were already famous to the general public. I was an exception. As an adopted child of stars, I already had my own fan clubs, my own mini-celebrity, and my own little embarrassing flings with fame. Some of the students resented me; they felt my popularity was "undeserved": I was just here because I was adopted into the lifestyle.

I drove slowly, rounding the five-acre, tree-lined campus. Typically, everyone has his or her car valeted; but today, not wishing to face anyone yet, I drove my yellow Mini Cooper into the underground garage and parked it myself.

"Too embarrassed to valet today, huh?" A snide voice rang out from behind me as I got out of my car.

I didn't even need to turn around to know who it was. The distinctive nasal, high-pitched squeal gave it away. My shoulders slumped as I turned to face Stacey Macedo, dressed in an electric blue paisley top, white head wrap, and leggings. She stood a few feet away, directly across from me, with her hips cocked at a menacing angle.

Stacey was exactly the kind of resentful Newton student I was talking about. She'd been working since second grade to break into the entertainment industry. Her parents owned a chain of fast-food restaurants and were filthy rich in their own right. They were important people, to be sure, but unable to provide Stacey with direct access to the red carpet of fame.

I'd call Stacey my archnemesis, but that might justify her cause, so I usually just tried to ignore her. Being the bigger woman is good karma, or so I'm told.

"Nope," I said, closing my car door. "Just didn't feel like waiting in line." Adjusting my specially dyed chiffon ruffle blouse, I walked past her toward the elevator.

"So, Caroline Treasure and your dad? You know everyone knew about them anyway, right? It's *so* last week's news already," she said, an evil smirk on her face as she followed me.

"Mmhmm," I said, knowing she was just trying to get a rise out of me. Unfortunately, I hadn't really planned out how I was going to handle this unwanted attention today, and getting pissed off wasn't an option. I jammed the UP button with the palm of my hand.

"It's just so sad when guys cheat, isn't it?" she said teasingly. "Or when a woman can't keep track of her man."

I twirled around. "Hey, Stace, how's that pilot you tried out for last month? Hear anything back from them yet?" I knew the television show she tried out for hadn't even been a pilot; it was just a shooting test so they could entice a real actress to try out for the part. "I heard they're going in another direction. Did they even bother telling you?"

Stacey's glossy green eyes grew wide. "Well, if I was a talentless—"

The elevator door opened, cutting her off. Rachelle appeared magically before us, pulled me in, and then promptly hit the CLOSE button before a surprised Stacey could recover.

"Thank God you're here." I smiled at my savior. "You prove, yet again, why you're so amazing."

Rachelle snapped back her head in a princess-of-power pose

and beamed. "I know, I know, your heroine. I saw your car skip the valet and ran to meet you here."

Outfitted in a miniskirt, large hoop earrings, and a top I recognized as Fred Segal, my heroine would have given Wonder Woman a run for her money. Rachelle's mom is Evangelina Torres, singer, part-time model, and the face of Avalon Cosmetics. Rachelle inherited her mom's pouty lips, curvaceous body, and trademark strut.

"Thanks, I totally owe you one."

"Oooh, how about I just borrow this instead?" she said, noticing my new charm bracelet.

"Good try."

She shrugged in mock defeat. "So, what was that all about?"

"Oh, you know, the usual. She hates me; she tries to make me feel bad; she says something nasty; I try to ignore it."

"That girl needs to get over it. Everyone's more famous and popular than she is. She just has to deal!" We laughed as the elevator zipped us to the second floor.

In moments like these, Rachelle and I got along fabulously. We made fun of the same things (she was a bit more open about it, though), we got each other's pop culture references, and we loved to shop together. Sure, she could be a bit flakey and a little self-centered, and she annoyed me sometimes; but we've been best friends since our nannies set us up on a play date when we were two years old.

"Your mom called my mom yesterday. Your dad's a total jerk, huh?"

Flinching at her choice of words, I nodded weakly.

"Do you want to talk about it now?" The doors to the elevator opened, and we stepped into the bustling hallway. "Or do you want to hear about my big date yesterday?"

I did want to talk to her about the divorce, but there were way too many people around. Everyone was already looking at me as it was.

"Rain check on one, immediately on two. C'mon, walk me to English."

"Okay, so, last night was magical. I went for an evening drive with Marc Laurence, and he took me to the cutest little spot on a hill overlooking the city. We stayed there for hours just talking, listening to music, and, well, you know."

"Are you serious? *Marc Laurence?*" I expected Rachelle to know better. That particular hill was known as Marc's Hill, and what Rachelle had just fallen for was Marc's Infamous Romantic Date. Then again, Marc Laurence was probably the most coveted junior at school, so there were scores of young girls who had fallen for a similar top-down drive and subsequent make out session.

"I know, cute, isn't he? Here's the thing. After we started making out, I was seriously turned off. It turns out he's kind of a sloppy kisser. Totally gross."

I was a bit surprised. "Even with all that experience?"

"Terrible." She sounded pretty disappointed. "And now he keeps texting me. I just need to ignore him and hope he goes away."

Actually, maybe I should feel sorry for Marc. Rachelle didn't only inherit her mom's killer body and stunning looks; she also acquired Evangelina's habit of shedding men on a whim. Marc was about to get taken for a ride on the Rachelle Torres roller coaster of love.

The bell rang for the first class.

"Ooops, I'm going to be late. Gotta go. See you later?" Rachelle said as she hurried down the hall.

I couldn't keep a silly grin from spreading over my face. "Sure, thanks, Rach."

As she clacked down the hall, she yelled back, "And, Chloe, we'll totally talk about your parents later!"

Sigh.

I forgot to mention, the one downside of being friends with Rachelle was that *discretion* was not in her vocabulary. Everything I told her tended to spread around the school pretty quickly—despite my best efforts to swear her to secrecy. It's hard to blame her, though. Rachelle's family used to star in a reality TV series called *The Stepfords*. So, privacy and discretion weren't exactly Rachelle's family's strong suit.

I walked into my English class and headed to the back row, pulling out my copy of *Variety* magazine. I was hoping to avoid talking to anyone. A minute later, Stacey slid into an empty chair next to me. Thankfully, yet oddly enough, she didn't acknowledge me.

As Mr. Ronstein called the class to attention, he paused and looked toward the back of the class. "Ms. Macedo, what are you doing here? I don't believe you're in this period."

I realized he was right. Stacey wasn't in this class. I had made sure not to be in any classes with her. Carrie Markin, one of Stacey's friends, started giggling three rows over. This could be trouble.

Stacey stood up. Every head was turned toward her in rapt attention. This was probably the biggest audience she was ever going to get. "Oh, I'm sorry, Mr. Ronstein. I just wanted to get Chloe's autograph really quick," she said in her most cloying voice.

Looking directly at me and uncapping a pen with one hand while reaching into her bag with the other, she held out a copy of *Celeb Weekly*. "Chloe, if you could, please? This will be worth so much more if you could just sign it." She gave me an evil grin.

My whole body stiffened, and I felt my face turn red-hot as snickers filled the room. Unbelievable! I didn't know Stacey would stoop so low.

Mr. Ronstein stepped toward us and took Stacey by the arm. "Ms. Macedo, you're going to have to leave now."

Clapping erupted as he guided Stacey out of the room. She practically curtsied out the door. I couldn't tell if people were clapping because she was getting in trouble or in support of her wicked deed. I sat stuck to my chair, shame replaced by rage.

I felt a light tap on my arm, and Leslie Stuart leaned over and said, "That was so totally not cool, Chloe. I'm really sorry." I looked over at her and noticed that on her desk was a copy of the same magazine. She saw me looking at it and sheepishly shut the magazine and tossed it into her backpack.

"Sorry."

There was no avoiding it. Even my allies couldn't help reading all about the divorce.

After making it through the rest of English and World History with no further incidents, I was relieved to have morning break. I headed out to the big tree on the lawn behind the vending machines. That was where the popular girls hung out. The senior girls would normally have to invite you to sit with them, and they usually didn't even give you a chance until you were at least a junior; but Rachelle and I had been preapproved since day one of sophomore year. I think between my pseudofame and Rachelle's outright hotness, they had no choice but to give us early admission.

As I approached, two of the regulars, Joanna and Ashley, were already sitting on the grass with what looked like a half dozen cupcakes laid out before them.

"Hey, what's up? Where's Rach?" they asked in unison.

I dropped down next to them. "I don't know. It's already been the worst morning ever."

Joanna shrugged as she licked some frosting off her fingers. She was the natural blonde of the two, but Ashley always dyed her strawberry-colored hair blonde anyway. They were high-end surfer chicks, meaning they were terribly fit, awesomely bronzed, and freckly from head to toe. They could have passed as sisters, especially since their fashion sense was practically identical. It was Roxy hoodies and clunky sandals for both today, with an aquamarine tank top for Ashley and a plain white baby-tee for Joanna.

"Here, have a cupcake. It'll make everything better." Ashley smiled and handed me one. "Everyone's voting on whether Sprinkles or SusieCakes is better. Try this and tell me what you think."

The students of Newton, being far more than just attendees at an exclusive private school, didn't just get complimentary milk during morning break. They were pushing for three-dollar cupcakes too.

"Ooooh, not bad. Kinda dense," I said, biting into one. It did make me feel better. I reached for another. "Where's the milk?"

Ashley said, "It's all gone. Brit's running down to the middle school to get some."

"She's stealing milk from the middle schoolers?"

"Hey, people did it to us when we were that age. I figure we're due," Ashley mumbled in between bites. "It's either that or go buy a soda."

"I'll go get a soda then," I said, wiping my hands on the grass. As I got up to leave, Ashley said, "Wait, why's it been the worst morning ever?"

"Two words: Stacey Macedo."

She nodded knowingly.

Joanna added, "Hey, by the way, sorry about your parents. Sucks to hear. I hope you're alright."

"I'm okay. I'll catch you guys later. Thanks for the cupcakes."

"Cool, see you later." Thumbs-up and a peace sign from both.

I popped around the corner and headed for the vending machine.

"Hey," Austin said, running up to me. I turned around to find him smiling as if yesterday never happened.

I rolled my eyes, grabbed my Diet Coke, and headed off toward the music building, pretending he didn't even exist.

"Chloe, slow down a second," he said, stepping next to me and matching me stride for stride.

Secretly, I did want to hear what he had to say, even if I had mentally purged him from my life last night. I slowed down just a little but kept my eyes staring straight ahead. "Oh, now you're ready to say something to me? You didn't even say good-bye yesterday."

"Look, I'm sorry. I was all pissed off about basketball practice and everything," he said, sounding really apologetic. "I just found out about your dad this morning."

Turning to face him, I narrowed my eyes. "Listen, I was trying to tell you about it yesterday, but you—"

"Weren't paying attention. I know, I know. Like I said, it was basketball, okay? We have a big game coming up and Coach was on my ass and, really, how could I have known?"

"Austin! I was crying on the phone. What did you think I was crying about?"

"I don't know. You kind of cry a lot." He shrugged. "Listen, I'm just trying to say I'm sorry. I want to make it up to you. It must have been terrible for you yesterday, and I'm sorry I was a part of that. I should have been supportive."

The magic words. I hate how I can't stay angry at someone for a long time. As he kept talking ("I was wrong, totally wrong.") I couldn't help noticing how great he looked today. Or how comfortable it'd be nestling into that spot right on his perfect chest.

"What about Josie?" I heard myself say.

"Oh, come on. She's nothing compared to you. I was just trying to, you know, get your attention." That's funny. That's what I was trying to do by breaking up with him in the first place. I didn't tell him that, of course.

"So, what about it? I'll call you later and we'll do something? My dad may be able to get tickets to a basketball game—courtside seats."

I paused. "No promises, but you can call me later."

He reached out for a hug and then leaned in to steal a kiss. Sneaky, sneaky. I couldn't help it and gave him a quick kiss back.

Maybe this day was destined to get better.


A few minutes later, I opened the door to Flower Auditorium and immediately searched for Vickie Strauss, the only reason I looked forward to music class at all. Vickie's situation was sort of weird. She was the third daughter of Vanessa Gale, one of the biggest pop icons of the eighties, but she wasn't popular at all in school despite being a certified star brat. Vickie's two sisters had already gone through Celebrity High and made a mark for themselves. She was expected to do the same, but she lacked the confidence to really break out despite having a fabulous singing voice.

Today Vickie was sitting in our usual corner, absentmindedly chewing on the tips of her light brown hair as she looked at some kids messing with the piano. As soon as she saw me approach, she jumped up and ran over, giving me a huge hug. "Oh my gosh, are you okay? I just heard about your parents."

It was so easy to love Vickie. Unlike Rachelle, she always knew just what to say.

"I'm okay, I guess." I latched on to her arm comfortingly.

"I didn't expect you to be here."

"That afraid of hearing me sing, huh?"

She laughed. "Well, yeah, sort of. But seriously, my mom took me out of school for a few days when Dan first left us. She didn't want me to have to deal with a whole big scene at school. I thought your mom would've done the same."

"Yeah, I know. I've heard enough snickers and under-the-breath remarks already, and it's only eleven."

"Oh, I'm sure not everyone's talking about it that much, if it makes you feel better," she offered.

"Really? How'd you find out?"

Vickie flushed a little and paused. "Okay, fine, everyone is talking about it. I heard during homeroom from Kathy Resinger." She shrugged apologetically.

What a sweetie she was, trying to tell me not everybody was talking behind my back, even as the room exploded in excited whispers as people noticed me coming in.

"Okay, settle down and focus. We need to start rehearsals for the musical, and I want us to be perfect!" Mrs. O'Shea, the new music teacher, hushed the crowd by clapping her hands for attention.

The most important weeks of school at Celebrity High weren't finals or midterms. The most stressful times of the year were the weeks leading up to the winter talent show and the end-of-the-year musical. As you'd imagine, with all the celebrity-spawned talent prima donna-ing around, the competition for the leads in these musicals could get pretty intense.

The previous year's musical, *The Sound of Music: Remix*, had been a fiasco, culminating in the firing of our music teacher. After accepting a particularly tasty bribe from the family of Madeline Simone, the teacher had reneged on his end of the deal. Madeline not only failed to secure the lead role of Maria; she didn't even get to play Leisl, despite being a spitting image of the blue-eyed beauty.

The Simones waited until opening night to go public with their anger, attempting to pull a coup d'état by locking poor Vickie, now playing the lead role, in her dressing room before the show started. When Madeline bounded onstage for the first scene, chaos ensued and the whole dirty story came out. The production was canceled, the teacher was fired, Madeline was transferred, and Vickie was given next year's female lead in return.

Unfortunately for her, this year's selection was *Footloose: The Musical*, and Vickie couldn't dance or keep a beat, so she was relegated to the chorus. Since I couldn't sing a lick and hadn't been able to convince Mrs. O'Shea that the play would be better off with me as a jovial, mute tree, I was stuck in the chorus too.

On the positive side of things, Vickie and I became pretty good friends, and she gave me a good-humored elbow whenever I started getting a bit too enthusiastic with my off-key rendition of "Let's Hear It For the Boy."

"Ugh. You should've seen what Stacey did in English class," I whispered as Mrs. O'Shea started class. "Totally humiliated me."

"No way," Vickie said, looking concerned. "She needs to finally get some starring role somewhere so she can stop making everyone else's life just as miserable as her own."

"Yeah, I—"

"CHLOE-GRACE." We hadn't even noticed that Mrs. O'Shea had stopped talking. "Chloe-Grace, could you come up here for a moment?"

Feeling the color rise to my cheeks, I looked at Vickie and then worked my way down to the front of the room, expecting to be reprimanded for talking. Instead, Mrs. O'Shea peered over her thick glasses and handed me a hall pass.

"Mrs. Wenter wants to see you. Bring your books, please." I retrieved my stuff; silently mouthed to Vickie, "I'll see you later"; and headed out the door.

Mrs. Wenter had been working here as a guidance counselor since I was in the seventh grade, and she'd always been a bit too nosy about my family life. Our guidance talks would inevitably turn toward the topic of how my parents were doing, what kinds of parties we were throwing, or even what the inside scoop on my next birthday celebration might be. I suspected she had called me in today for more than just some friendly counseling.

"Chloe-Grace! There you are! I'm really excited to see you." She sounded overeager, as usual, dramatically twirling around in her high leather chair to face me.

Entering Mrs. Wenter's office is like walking into a third-rate Planet Hollywood. Pictures of stars on the walls, autographed and alphabetized; knock-off memorabilia peeking out from every shelf; and a vanity photograph of a younger Mrs. Wenter hanging in a heavy, gilded frame behind her.

Time to cue up the excitement. "Hey, Mrs. Wenter! Good to see you too; I love your new haircut. You look amazing." This was the safest thing to say to her, because she was always getting her hair cut. "So, am I in trouble or something?"

"Oh no, nothing's wrong at all. Go ahead and close the door for me." She directed me forward into the room. "Have a seat."

I was pretty sure Mrs. Wenter wanted to ask me about my parents' divorce, so I figured I'd better try to distract her.

"Mrs. Wenter, if this is about gym class last week, I really was sick. I'm allergic to polyester and grass makes me woozy, so I thought it was best if I sat out."

"No, no. That's fine. It's just, I heard about your parents and thought that maybe you'd like to talk about it."

Crap, plan A down the tubes.

Mrs. Wenter pulled out a blank notebook from her desk

drawer and continued, "It's not normally our business to pry, but we know how these things can be for our students. Divorces are hard, especially when another woman is involved—and it's all over the tabloids. I just thought maybe you'd like to talk."

"No, I'm fine. Really. It's—"

"Did you know this was coming?" she interrupted. A pen had suddenly materialized in her hand, and it was practically dripping with anticipation. It was clear I was going to have to talk about this.

"Um, not really." I shrugged. That was honest, I didn't know at all. "I mean, I just found out about all this yesterday."

"This must be so hard on you, then. How are you feeling, how is your mom doing, and where's your dad right now? Don't be afraid to let it all out." I could see that this line of questioning was going exactly where I didn't want it to.

Well, as my mom always said, "When in doubt, cry." Since I was nine years old, I'd been perfecting the over-the-top-yet-emotionally-convincing cry.

"Well, you know, it's just been so hard." A little stream of tears started down my face, and Mrs. Wenter stopped scribbling on her pad.

"Now, um, if you need a few moments, I understand." Mrs. Wenter pushed a box of tissues across the table toward me.

Throwing my hands to my face, I started sobbing, and Mrs. Wenter signaled a full retreat. Five minutes of my histrionic crying and half a box of tissues later, she said uncomfortably, "Um, okay, so maybe, um, I think it would be okay if you went home for the rest of the day."

I sniffled into the last of the tissues and whimpered softly for dramatic effect.

"This is clearly a bad time for us to talk. I'll get someone to take you home."

"Yes, I'd better go home."

"Mr. Benson can do it, I'm sure." The school custodian? Why in the world would the *custodian* take me home?

I wiped my hand across my eyes, ruining the rest of my make-up job. "It's okay; I should be fine to drive. Don't worry about it, Mrs. W. I'll just take a moment to collect myself." I was already patting myself on the back for an Oscar-winning performance and preparing for an afternoon of decompressing by my pool.

Mrs. Wenter got up from her desk and walked over to the windows. "Actually, I'm not worried about your ability to drive home, Chloe. I'm worried about them," she said, as she pulled open the blinds with a flourish.

Blinding light filled the room; and after a few blurry moments, I focused on three television trucks, two dozen photographers, and a handful of reporters gathered by the entrance to the school. It looked as if Mr. Benson, our janitor, was playing security guard, yelling at the crowd. He was trying to prevent the photographers from snapping pictures by waving his hands in front of their cameras.

"Wow, how long have they been out there?"

Mrs. Wenter sounded frustrated. "About thirty minutes. Did you notice anyone following you to school today?"

"Uh, not really. I wasn't paying attention, though. It's kind of been a long morning."

"Of course. Well, they're here now and waiting for you." She tapped the pen against her forehead. "You can't be seen leaving. They'll never leave you alone."

Wow, was she actually concerned for me? "We'll tell them that you weren't at school today. Hopefully they'll go away and then Mr. Benson can take you home." Seeing the confused look on my face again, Mrs. Wenter quickly added, "We have to have someone else drive you home. They'll know your car, of course. They won't follow Mr. Benson at all."

She had a good point, actually. But then again, thinking quickly, I had a much better idea. "Hey, Mrs. W., how about this idea. . . ."

Ten minutes later I was at Rachelle's locker, watching her color match one of the many wigs she keeps on hand to my hair. Wigs in her locker? Yeah, that's Rachelle. She had half her wardrobe in her locker. Or rather, in lockers. She rents locker space from people around her; and at any given time, she is leasing three to five lockers for her various costumes and getups. Most people dressed in the mornings at home, but Rachelle thinks it makes sense to have outfits available at school to change into after surveying her mood for the day. The wigs are there to complement whatever outfit she chooses. Today, however, they were to serve a higher purpose: to disguise Rachelle as me so I could slip away from school unseen.

I had naively hoped that roping Rachelle into this gig would allow us to spend a gorgeous afternoon tanning, but Rachelle was taking this way too seriously. "What do you think about this one? I like it, but I'm not sure I can style it like you did your hair today. Cute, by the way. Maybe this one will work. . . ."

"Rachelle, it doesn't matter which wig you pick," I said, itching to get this show on the road. "You don't even need one. You're just going to drive my car. Nobody's going to see you."

"*Nobody's going to see me?* Are you crazy? You asked for a distraction; I'm going to give you a proper distraction. Nobody's going to see me. Hilarious." Rachelle settled on a wig and started adjusting the fit in her locker's wide-screen mirror.

"Give me your top. And jacket." She was already taking off her metallic blouse, revealing a crepe camisole underneath. I slipped off my top and handed it over. Of course, once Rachelle put on my top and jacket, they looked a hundred times better on her than they had on me. Typical.

Mr. Benson, Mrs. Wenter, and I waited next to my car in the school's underground garage and watched impatiently as Rachelle climbed in. "How do I look?" she asked as she rolled down the driver's-side window, put on her seatbelt, and adjusted my rearview mirror.

"You look just like me, but hotter. Remember, just drive around for a while and then meet me back at my house."

Without another glance at us, Rachelle revved the engine harder than I would have liked and hurtled out of the garage. The crowd gathered there realized that the car wasn't stopping or slowing down, so they quickly parted as the yellow blur screeched out through the gates and sped away down the main road.

A few of the more astute paparazzi pointed at my car and yelled, "That's her!" In a scramble to catch up, all the cameramen and reporters ran to their cars and peeled out after the quickly disappearing Mini. In two minutes tops, the crowd was fully dispersed, and everyone was following Rachelle-Chloe to who knows where.

"Okay, Chloe. Let's go!" We walked to the school van. "But I think you should crouch down in the back of the van as we sneak out through the gates. Just so no one sees you," Mr. Benson said, buying into his accomplice role a little too much.

"Uh, okay," I said, hesitantly crawling in between buckets and cleaning solvents as he closed the back of the van and climbed into the driver's seat.

The leisurely pace at which he was driving wasn't going to get me home before I puked from the smell of dirty buckets and chemicals. Sick of holding my breath for what seemed like hours, I gasped out, "Um, Mr. Benson? Can I come up front now? It's, like, really gross back here, and I feel sick."

I wasn't sure he heard me, but then he started looking furtively around and checking all the mirrors. He finally motioned me into the passenger seat. I scrambled up there as fast as I could and cranked the window halfway down for some fresh air.

Suddenly panicked, Mr. Benson reached across and opened the glove compartment. Two lighters, a flutter of receipts, and a pair of horrendous plastic orange-rimmed sunglasses spilled out.

Without taking his eyes off the road, he said, "You should probably put those on if you're going to have the window down." The windows in the van weren't even tinted. This was easily the weirdest ride I'd ever accepted. I humored him and put on the glasses.

"Nobody will recognize you now," Mr. Benson said, seeming satisfied that he'd done his job in whisking me away safely.

I smiled, and we sat there awkwardly in silence for about ten minutes.

"You know, I used to have posters of your mom in my room."

My eyes got really wide in shock. This was getting a little uncomfortable.

"She was just so beautiful."

I couldn't think of a single appropriate thing to say back, so I opted to stare in front of me and pray this ride was almost over.

"Really gorgeous," he continued. "But it's odd. The two of you don't really look alike."

Mr. Benson obviously wasn't too smart.

I sighed.

Wonderful. I guess my day wasn't meant to get better.

# Chapter
## 3

"Mom! You home?" I yelled, running in through the front door as the van pulled away.

"Chloe, what're you doing here?" Her voice buzzed over the intercom. "It's only noon. Shouldn't you be at school?"

I assumed she was still in bed, so I headed upstairs. When I threw open the door, I was surprised to see that she wasn't there.

"Chloe? Where are you?" the intercom buzzed again.

"In your room, where are you?"

"I'm in the garden with David." Her voice sounded stressed-out, even over the intercom.

I ran back downstairs and made my way into the oval-shaped garden. My mom was already fully dressed and relaxing on a divan. Pink cashmere tank, white half coat buttoned only at the top, and custom-made candy cane UGGs. Yes, it sounds ridiculous, but she can somehow pull it off.

David, mom's publicist, was hovering nearby; and it looked as if he was talking on two phones at once. He gave me a little nod and then stepped around the corner.

"Why are you home, darling? Did you forget something?" my mom said as I approached her.

"No, they just sent me home because there's too much press outside the school. They said they were going to give you a call when I left."

Extending her arms into a movie star caricature of a yawn, she said, "We've been avoiding the phones all morning. David's still trying to figure out how to spin this before we speak with anyone."

David suddenly clicked both phones closed. Turning around dramatically, he looked at me. "Chloe, it's a good thing you're here," he said, running his hand through his slicked-back black hair. "The photographers are coming in a few hours. We're going to need to take some photos of you and your mom hanging around the house."

He paused to take a look at my outfit.

"And you're going to have to change out of that. You don't really match." I looked down. I'd forgotten that I had switched Rachelle's blouse for my ruffled one. "Try to put on something a little less obvious."

While David was a fabulous publicist, having no life aside from ours made him kind of out of touch with the niceties of the human race. But despite his idiosyncrasies, David always knew what to do and could subtly fend off negative press by pushing it in another direction (he kept a file of negative things other celebrities did, ready to send off at any time) or by doing what he was aiming for today: creating a positive image for the press.

"We're going to need as many shots as possible of the two of you around the house. It has to look like you've been having the time of your lives around here, without your dad." He turned to me. "Go see if you have any great pictures of just you and your mom lying around somewhere. Anything we can use. We'll leak those out and set the idea that your mom is your main caretaker and deserves full custody of you."

"What? Custody? Mom, what—" They were already discussing who gets custody of me? Wasn't I going to be asked about this?

"Chloe, you heard David; run along now."

"Um, okay. Be right back." I couldn't deal with this right now. I headed to the kitchen for a snack, but the sudden squealing of tires on the driveway alerted me that Rachelle had arrived. I went out the front door just as she jerked the Mini into a parked position.

"So, what took you so long?" I asked as she came up the steps. We walked into the kitchen, and I grabbed an apple and some peanut butter.

"Well, you know I just had to get out of the car and give them an interview, didn't I?" She slid on to a counter stool across from me. "They seemed pretty upset when I took off the wig, so I wanted to make it up to them."

I laughed and almost choked. "Of course. Passing up a photo op would have been so out of character for you."

"Naturally."

"So, what did you say?"

"As your official and lifelong best friend, I felt it was my responsibility to speak for you. I said that you were distressed and hurt, and that you wanted to have some time to figure things out. I told them to direct all questions to me and that we'd be in constant contact during this difficult and troubling time."

"I'm surprised you didn't pass out your phone number and set up a gossip hotline."

"Oh please, I am so the Fort Knox of secrets." She flashed me a winning smile that would have easily convinced anyone else, but I knew better.

"Well, thanks, Rach. If only you could be me all the time, I could be you and have sloppy make outs with Marc Laurence while you dealt with the annoying reporters."

Tossing her hair for absolutely no reason, she sighed. "Trust me, I'd rather do that any day of the week than make out with Marc again." She stuck out her tongue and fake gagged. "So, what's going on?" she said, reaching a delicate finger directly into the peanut butter jar and scooping out a bite. "I saw David being all Tyra-like over there. The divorce is really happening?"

My okay mood immediately dropped. "Well, I guess my mom sort of knew about Caroline Treasure already. So yeah, the divorce is happening."

"I'm sorry," Rachelle said, softening her voice "That kinda sucks." She paused to lick her finger clean. "Then again, of course she knew. Everyone knew about your dad and Caroline Treasure."

"Wait. What? You knew about this? How come everyone knew about this but me?"

Rachelle reached out for another scoop. I mock-slapped her hand away and pulled a little spoon out of the drawer for her to use.

"Sure, well, not knew knew. But I read about it on a blog or something. They were rumored to be seeing each other. You didn't see that?"

"I try not to read those things. They're never true, anyway." Maybe I should be reading some gossip blogs. Apparently I was missing out on important information.

"Well, *this* one turned out to be true. If it's any consolation, your dad was rumored to be with a couple of different girls; Caroline Treasure was just one of them."

"Um, thanks, Rach. How is that supposed to make me feel better? And how come you didn't tell me about it then?"

She shrugged lightly. "I dunno; it was just Hollywood gossip. To be honest, I figured you never brought it up because you didn't want to talk about it. I wasn't going to push you if you didn't bring it up. Right to privacy, you know?"

"I guess, but you still should have told me."

"Well, say I told you I was reading about all these things. And then you ask your mom or dad, and the rumors don't turn out to be true. Then what? I make you all worried for nothing. I'm just looking out for you, Chlo." This time her smile was hard to resist.

Rolling my eyes, I gave up. "Fine. But next time you read something about my family, just be sure to tell me, okay?"

"Sure, no problem."

"C'mon, let's go upstairs. I have to find some pictures for David."

We headed to my room, and I dug around in a drawer to find some old photos. I didn't really feel like sifting through them to see which ones contained just me and my mom, so I set a pile aside. I ducked into my walk-in closet to look for some appropriate candid photo outfits to change into and pulled out an extralong blue sweater tunic and a pair of white jeans.

Rachelle grabbed my laptop and jumped on the bed. "Mind if I log on?" Her fingernails were already clacking on the keyboard as she asked. I knew exactly where she was headed. Rachelle's got an addiction to the Internet. Well, not the Internet exactly. She's addicted to news about herself, but the Internet kind of facilitates that. If you look through her search history, it's got things such as "Rachelle Torres hot" and "Rachelle Torres star" listed. It's kind of gross if you think about it; but to be honest, I do the same thing— sometimes.

"Check it out; they're already calling this the fourth-biggest divorce Hollywood's ever seen."

"Who's the first three?"

"Well, Britney and K-Fed, Brad and Jennifer, and then Lucy and Desi—heard of them?"

"You don't know who Lucille Ball and Desi Arnaz are?"

"Nope, should I?"

Looking in the mirror for a final check through, I gave her an incredulous stare. "For all the TV you watch, you've never seen *I Love Lucy*?"

"What is that? Is it on Wednesdays?" She was distracted and completely lost in her Facebook page.

"Forget it. Let's go. Grab those pictures for me, will you?"

We headed downstairs and walked into the living room, where David, my mom, and the camera crew were setting up. For a candid photo shoot, there sure was a lot of equipment involved. Even Luther, Mom's longtime stylist and makeup designer, had been called in.

As my mom sat in a chair in a new outfit and Manolo heels, he buzzed around her applying makeup and chattering the entire time. "Dominique, you really need to stop going out in the sun. It's going to absolutely ruin your face."

Dabbing at her cheeks with a sponge, he added, "I mean *ruin* like only ninety out of a hundred women would want to look like you." Working with Luther would make anybody feel absolutely beautiful, if only because he told you every five seconds.

He stopped rumpling Mom's hair long enough to give me and Rachelle a quick wave and an appraising glance. "Don't you two just look like perfection squared."

David noticed us come in too. "Chloe, there you are. Let's get ready to take a few shots of you and your mom watching TV together. We'll start with the two of you sitting here." He patted the crook of the couch. "Just lounge around a bit. Someone go get a bowl of popcorn or something. And put some drinks on the table."

It wasn't exactly the most comfortable and relaxed atmosphere. We were posed and then told to relax. Which doesn't sound that difficult in theory, but it's not easy to do. We took a few shots pretending it was a lazy Friday night and we were home, just the two of us, watching a movie. David previewed the digital pictures on the computer and didn't like them, so we did it again. "We need you guys to be a bit more natural. Let's actually put on something and you guys just watch it. Chloe, forget we're here; relax a little. It looks forced." *Of course it was forced,* I thought, *I was fake watching TV.*

I couldn't focus on the television because I kept getting distracted by Rachelle doing random poses in the dining room, our next location, while they checked the lighting in there. It looked as if she was flirting with one of the cameramen while he was furiously firing away with his camera and laughing right back.

David noticed the laughing and watched Rachelle and the cameraman interact for a moment. "Hey, Rachelle, come over here a sec."

She blew one last kiss at the camera and sauntered over to David. "Need something?"

"Yeah, let's have you go on the couch next to Chloe. Pretend like you're just hanging out, watching a movie. . . ."

Before he had even finished the sentence, Rachelle had dropped onto the couch next to me, grabbed the remote, stuffed a handful of popcorn in her mouth, and looked as if she'd been there for hours.

I tried to emulate her, but I just ended up slouching too much and felt like a deflated couch potato. Rachelle's natural grace—even while pretending to watch TV—made David forget how awkward I looked. I wasn't sure how they were going to label these pictures: "Family time at home. With friend." Great. They might as well just cut me out for all the sense of family these pictures would have.

David took a look at the new set of pictures and gave a quick nod of approval. "That looks beautiful. Let's move on to the dining room." The crew immediately started to shift over.

Rachelle hooked her arms through mine and my mom's as we got up from the couch. "You guys look amazing. Seriously, these pictures are going to be perfect!"

I couldn't even say anything because I knew they would . . . now.

Luther busted in from stage left with his travel makeup kit in hand and disentangled me from Rachelle. "I'm going to adjust Chloe's look real quick. We'll be right back."

Whisking me into the bathroom, he half shut the door and started unpacking his instruments of glamour from his bag.

As he started to slap on foundation and cake on the blush, I began to worry. "Luther, shouldn't we look natural? Like we're at home? Isn't that the point?"

Without missing a brushstroke, Luther looked right into my eyes. "Honey, what's bothering you? You've got two minutes. Go." Before I could even open my mouth to respond, he said, "It's Rachelle, isn't it? She's not even supposed to be in the pictures. That's what you're thinking."

"Sort of. I don't really mind, but you know, I thought this was supposed to be a family picture."

Luther nodded knowingly. "Listen, I'll distract her. It really shouldn't be that hard. Something shiny—a new lipstick, something like that. You go take over those pictures."

Even as he said this, I knew it wasn't fair.

"Actually, Luther, it's not really Rachelle. I mean, it's fine she's in these pictures, I guess." I didn't want to make it seem as if I was upset with Rachelle, since I really wasn't.

Luther stopped with his impromptu makeover and took a step back to survey the scene. "So, it's something else? Stop tearing. You can't cry; I won't allow it. You'll ruin my work. Tell me what's really going on." He started gently dabbing around my eyes with a cotton ball.

"Well, this whole photo shoot thing. It's just so . . . contrived. When was the last time my mom and I sat around watching a movie?"

Luther nodded knowingly. "Well, your mom has been really busy recently, you know. Maybe it feels fake, but it's something she needs you to do for her right now. Just try to get through it; help her out, and you'll feel better."

"I know, but—"

"It's not easy being an actress, you know. You wouldn't believe how much time it takes to get a movie made. Look at me; I don't have any time to myself, and I'm just the stylist. Trust me, your mom is always talking about how much she misses you. She always has. How do you think I always know everything that's going on with you?"

"What's going on with me?"

"She told me you're doing amazing in school, just like you always have. She's really proud of that, you know."

"So, does my mom talk about my dad a lot?" I asked, seizing an opportunity to see if Luther knew how my parents actually got along.

"Of course she does. All the time. About how she has no idea what he's doing, how frustrated she is with his total inability to finish his album, and how often she wishes he would just do something."

"So, like, they've been having problems."

"Honey, everyone has problems. Even I have problems, and I'm the happiest person I know." He smiled.

It was true; Luther was pretty much the happiest person I knew. It hadn't occurred to me that maybe he wasn't this way all the time. "What problems do you have?"

"Shush now. I never kiss-and-tell." Luther winked at me so ridiculously, I had to laugh.

"Really? And you won't tell me about it?"

"What? My little problems? Please, you've got so much going on right now."

Before I could continue, David's voice rang out. "Chloe, hurry up! Luther! Get her in here!"

With a smile, Luther put down the eyelash curler. "Go take those pictures. You look gorgeous." He deposited me in the dining room and turned to Rachelle. "Girl, come with me; you need some of this magic touch."

Never one to turn down a fuss-over-Rachelle session, Rachelle obliged and left the room.

It did feel better to be all done up. We started the shoot, pretending to eat a "family" dinner. I looked at my mom. She looked tired, but only I could tell. She was absolutely stunning in her makeup and pantsuit.

So the divorce was happening, and I had to deal. And Luther was right. Helping my mom would make me, and her, feel better.

I took a look at some of the dining-room pictures, and they looked okay. We could apparently fake eat together like a normal family. However, I was reaching the limit of my photo-taking patience, so when the doorbell rang I jumped up.

"I'll get it!" I yelled, running to the front of the house.

Yanking the door open in a rush, I stopped dead in my tracks and gasped.

*"Ohmigod, Dad?"*

# Chapter
## 4

"Hey, Chloe. Where's your mother?" he slurred, stumbling through the front door. My obviously drunken dad had a bouquet of wilted flowers in one hand and was supporting himself against the door with the other. Camera flashes were going off from behind him as I stood there, my mouth agape.

My dad had come to apologize the only way he knew how, by making a spectacle of the moment and bringing the entire cast and crew of *Entertainment NOW!* with him. I could imagine the lead-in and headlines already. This wasn't going to be pretty.

My dad's arms came forward in an awkward semicircle as he stumbled across the entryway. "Chloe! Come here and give me a hug," he burped out.

Repelled by the stench, I involuntarily took a step back as he slipped and fell.

"Dad!" I instinctively lunged forward to help him.

"John! Chloe! Stop right there! Don't touch her!" My mom

shrieked from somewhere behind me and I stood, frozen in place.

"Chloe, come here."

I looked back at her, standing strong and stately and beckoning for me to come to her side.

Glancing through the still-wide-open door, I could see the cameras creeping closer. I looked at both of my parents and said, "Mom, Dad, please, don't . . ."

Propped up against the wall, my dad echoed, "Yeah, Dominique, don't." He smiled.

I didn't see as much as hear Mom close the distance from the dining room to the front door in a frenzied rush. Her heels clacked purposefully across the marble floor as she blew by me toward my still-smiling father. At the last second she gathered herself and then sumo-shoved him up and out the door.

I let out a gasp.

Landing flat on his back, my dad was too stunned to react, just like the rest of us. While he lay there, sprawled out on the front steps, the flowers now lying destroyed across his chest, she swung back her right foot and then bent it into his Beckham.

I cringed, and a gasp erupted from the crowd of photographers, who paused for just a split second before resuming their picture taking.

Slamming the door behind her, my mom whipped around. Rachelle, David, Luther, and I stood there dumbfounded.

"Okay, so where were we?" she said, taking a deep breath.

After the longest dramatic pause ever, Luther said, "Hon, I think we might want to redo your hair and makeup."

David chimed in. "Dominique, I really wish you hadn't done that. Tomorrow is going to be hell."

"He deserved it," she said, smoothing down her hair. "And he was about to grab Chloe."

She looked over at me for agreement. I stood there, wide-eyed, too afraid to say anything. If being stuck between my parents was going to be my future, I didn't want any part of it. It looked as if my mom wanted me to take her side, which, circumstances as they were, was definitely the right side; but I wasn't quite ready to forget about Dad.

I wish I had just given him a hug instead of backing up. Maybe that would have prevented tomorrow's headlines.

"Actually, I think we're done here," David said. "Let's pack it up and we'll finish some other time."

My mom looked at me. "Chloe, I'm sorry about that." She looked pretty composed and was totally calm and collected. "Are you okay?"

I nodded, not really sure what else to do.

"How about you and Rachelle go upstairs? We'll talk later."

Rachelle and I couldn't get out of there fast enough, and ran up the stairs. "Ohmigod," Rachelle exclaimed, as she jumped on my bed. "Your mom moves so fast in high heels. I've never seen anybody run that fast in heels before! And how she threw him out with, like, no effort. Do you think it's her core strength training? I have got to find out what kind of program she's on. Your dad weighs a lot, I'll bet. I wonder if I'll be able to do that to my husband someday."

I stretched out on the floor and stared up at the ceiling, still in total shock. Rachelle was being supportive in her own distracting way, as usual. But while she could only concentrate on what just happened, I was worried about what was *going* to happen. Clearly, if my mom just tossed my dad out in full view of the cameras, the next day was going to be a paparazzi extravaganza.

"Chloe, are you listening to me?"

I sighed. "What? Oh, yeah. Umm, I think it's this new diet she's been on. I've noticed her eating a lot of mangoes lately."

Rachelle started trying to do sit-ups while hanging off the bed. "Mangoes? Hmm, I'll have to try it out. But seriously, that was insane! Don't you think it was kind of dumb for your dad to bring by some pathetic flowers and think it would all be okay? If somebody cheated on me, they'd better bring more than flowers."

Yeah, it was a pretty dumb move. The more I thought about it, the angrier I got. Was this just a publicity stunt for him? I mean, why would he bring all the paparazzi in the first place?

"You know," Rachelle continued, "once, on episode twelve of our show—I'm not sure if you remember it—they made my mom kick a guy out of our house after a bad date. It was a setup, though, since the producers thought it'd be more dramatic if she screamed at him and then slammed the door in his face. Today was kind of like that. . . ."

"Yeah, except this was not a setup." *This was my life.*

It all suddenly hit me, and I felt worn-out and defeated. Closing my eyes, I said, "Hey, Rach, I'm, like, supertired. Mind if we call it a day?"

"Sure, I should get home, anyway. I'll see you tomorrow," she said cheerily. "I can't wait to see the pictures!"

I smiled wanly. "Yeah, can't wait."

Few things are worth getting up for in the morning. Going to school the day after your mom publicly kicks your dad out of your house? That's the perfect reason to burrow under the covers and forget about everything.

With my alarm clock about to ring, I decided I was going to have to feign sickness quick.

As I heard my mom's heels on our hardwood floor, I pulled the covers up a bit more and put on my sick face.

"Chloe? What are you doing?"

I moaned weakly. "I'm not feeling that well, Mom. I think I'm coming down with something."

"You are feeling a little hot," she said, touching my forehead. "Well, that's probably good, because I didn't think you should go to school today, anyway. There's just too much craziness from yesterday."

"Really?" I suddenly perked up.

"I think we should probably talk about a few things," she said, walking over to pull the heavy curtains away from my windows. "I was going to do a little shopping and thought you might want to come along. If you're up to it, of course."

"Well, a shower would probably make me feel better."

Smiling knowingly, she headed out the door. "Good girl. See you downstairs."

I slid out of bed and headed toward the bathroom. This was certainly a little weird. I mean, my mom wasn't exactly a stickler for attending school every day, but for her to be up so early and to suggest we go shopping? Something was going on here. Then again, why ask too many questions when I'd just been offered a lifeline to avoid the drama that would have been the school day? Who knows when they were going to show the footage from yesterday. With my luck, it had probably already aired. I could just picture Stacey Macedo standing by my locker, pretending to fiddle with her books while waiting to deliver whatever stupid one-liner she had been working on all morning. Hallelujah for shopping.

One magical healing shower later, I put on my coral and gray striped halter top, a pair of skinny jeans, and my silver Chanel flats.

My mom was already in the car with the engine running by the time I got downstairs. I guess she hadn't bothered to call the driver. She certainly seemed like a woman on a mission.

"So, where we going?" I asked, getting in the car.

"I'm thinking we're going to need some coffee and then we'll head over to South Coast Plaza?"

My smile reluctantly transformed into a yawn. "Sure, sounds good. But is it even open yet?" It was barely a quarter past eight.

"Good point." The car swerved a little as she dug inside her purse with one hand. Pulling out her cell phone, she tossed it to me. "Call Marie and tell her we're going to want a few of the usual stores opened, but she doesn't have to worry about making them private."

I hit speed dial for my mom's personal shopper. She usually arranged for stores to be closed to the public before my mom went in. Apparently she was equally capable of having stores opened early too.

Marie sounded a bit groggy after picking up on the second ring. After a quick request relay, I covered the mouthpiece with my hand. "Marie wants to know if you want her to meet us there."

"Tell her we're fine. It'll just be the two of us today."

The day was getting stranger by the minute. After picking up our double nonfat lattes at the Coffee Shop's drive-through, my mom peeled out onto the street as a slurp of coffee sloshed onto the edge of the cup holder. Thirty minutes of frenzied driving later, we arrived at South Coast Plaza.

The mall was deserted as we walked over to our first stop of the day, Roberto Cavalli, one of my mom's favorites. Desiree, the store manager, had just arrived and was raising the metal security screen as we approached.

"Ms. Benjamin! How lovely to see you here. If you'll just give me a moment to get everything ready." She looked over at me. "And Chloe-Grace, you look darling today."

As we waited, I followed my mom as she browsed through one of the nearby racks.

"So, Mom, what're we looking for?"

"Oh, nothing in particular. I just thought maybe it would be nice to get out, just the two of us. We haven't done this in so long, you know."

This was definitely true. Going shopping together was something we used to do a lot when I was younger; but after mom's fame shot through the roof, she had her personal shoppers buy everything for her. Shopping with her was usually a huge production that involved tons of preplanning and an entourage, something I liked avoiding religiously.

Today, however, she wasn't being shy at all and delightfully declined any offers to close the store for a private shopping experience. Very odd for my mom. I watched her purposefully loiter near the big windows at the front, seemingly oblivious to onlookers. The mall started getting busier after an hour or so, and we began attracting a little parade of attentive fans as we went from store to store.

While riffling through a rack of dresses at Escada, my mom pulled out a shimmering gown. She waved me over excitedly. "Gorgeous, isn't it?" It was gorgeous but also pretty risqué, especially with the corseted top and the thigh-high split up the side. "Do you like it?"

"Um, it's nice?" I answered a little hesitatingly, because I wasn't sure what she meant by "Do *you* like it?"

"Great. Let's try it on, shall we?" Heading toward the dressing room, she asked Emma, the dressing room attendant, if they had one in a size zero. Okay, so it wasn't for me. Obviously.

"So, when are we going to talk about last night?" I asked as my mom tried on the gown and a string of other dresses.

My mom poked her head out of the dressing room. "Let me finish up here and we'll go get some food."

Thirty minutes and four dresses later we were sitting at Morendo in Santa Monica. My mom's mimosa had already gone through a refill, and I was slowly picking at my eggs Florentine.

"Did you know I tried to get your father to come do a movie with me?" Mom said, taking a quick sip of her drink. "He said he was a musician and not an actor." Laughing to herself, she continued, "Some musician he is. He hasn't done anything new in years. It's ridiculous, really. I'm going to cut him off. If he thinks he's getting anything from me, he's got another think coming."

"What do you mean by 'cut him off'?" I still held out a little bit of hope that they might work things out.

"I made him. He wouldn't even be famous if I hadn't married him." Taking off her sunglasses, she looked straight at me. "Your dad was a nobody when I met him. His career was going nowhere until we started dating."

That was only partially true. My dad was already up-and-coming, but certainly dating an A-list starlet had helped his cause. But that was besides the point. I was surprised to hear my mom disparage him like this. "That's a little harsh, Mom."

"I let him use my friends to book shows and concerts, and I dragged him everywhere with me." She chuckled again. "Look at him now. Where are all his fans? You know he was asked to be on one of those celebrity reality shows? God, how low can you go?"

"Mom, seriously, you're being really mean now. I know Dad was wrong, but still. What's going to happen?"

"Oh, Chloe, what do you think is going to happen? We're getting a divorce. I told the lawyer to get the paperwork started already. Do you know how this would look for my image if we stayed together?"

This was how my mom thought about things. Image was everything. It was probably because she'd been such a critic's darling for so long. She was the go-to actress for anything that required the beautiful but emotionally guarded love interest. She was used to playing the muse, the sophisticated ingenue, or the girl who remained faithfully behind while her man went off to war. When she had taken a role as a seductress in an indie movie, her performance had been ripped apart for being unbelievable and insulting to America's enchanted image of her.

Since then she'd been careful to always present herself in the best light, stretching her range at most to play the sassy but sweet female lead in crowd-pleasing romantic comedies. She wanted to make sure that the public would always perceive her in a positive and glamorous light.

I guess that's what she meant by *image*. Like people would look down on her for taking back her philandering husband. The problem was, what would happen to us, to me, if they didn't stay together? "Mom, what am I going to do?"

Looking surprised, she answered, "Stay with me of course. I

thought we already decided this. You can't go with your father now. I need you. And it wouldn't look right for you to take his side."

"Look right to who? This is our family, not a movie. And it's not really about taking sides, Mom, even though Dad was wrong." Which was definitely true. My dad had hurt my mom by cheating on her. "I'm just saying, shouldn't it be my decision?"

My mom's look of surprise turned to hurt. "Are you telling me you want to be with your dad after what he's done to me?"

"No, no. I mean, I definitely want to stay with you. It's just . . ." I put down my fork, done pretending to eat. "I haven't even talked to Dad yet. And I think we should. Or at least I should to get his side of the story."

My mom's eyes started to moisten, and she slumped back in her chair.

"I guess I should have seen this coming. You were always Daddy's little girl." She started dabbing at the corners of her eyes with a napkin. This was NOT how brunch was supposed to go.

"No, Mom! That's not what I meant! Look, I understand, okay? I won't talk to him if that's what you want. I'll wait for you guys to talk first. Just promise you'll talk to him? At least for me?"

If I was going to have to be in the middle of all this, maybe I could do some good. It didn't seem entirely crazy that maybe my dad had a reason for cheating on my mom. Maybe we weren't making him happy, or maybe he just made a stupid mistake. We had to give him a chance to explain, right?

"Fine, I'll talk to him," my mom said, nodding and partly recovering her composure. "Just don't let all this happen to you. Hopefully you'll never feel the pain I do right now. It's bad enough you have to see me like this."

A bit melodramatic—but that was Mom. At least she shed some insight into what was going on.

The rest of the day I spent by the pool, trying not to think about anything, while my mom took time to decompress from all the stress my dad was causing her (her words). After a few hours I headed inside for a makeshift dinner just as the doorbell rang.

"Um, hi," I said, opening the door to two hundred pounds of hotness, otherwise known as Chaynin Powers. I almost melted right there.

He smiled. "Hey, Chloe-Grace, how're you doing?"

*Ohmigod! Chaynin Powers knows my name!* I had a picture of him tacked onto my locker, dressed strategically in wife beater and jeans from his role in *Good Night, But Not Good-bye*, the movie that propelled him from nobody to one of the hottest young actors in Hollywood. Now he was here, standing right in front of me in all his physical glory.

"Is Dominique home?"

Oh, of course. He wasn't here to see me. What was I thinking? What would *Talk Magazine*'s Most Desirable Hollywood Bachelor have to do with me? Then again, what did he have to do with my mom? I didn't even know they knew each other.

"Umm, I'm not sure; let me check."

Chay grinned. "Cool, can I come in while you're checking?"

"Oh, right. Come in." I opened the door wide, and he breezed through, a whiff of cologne trailing him.

*Try to act casual, Chloe!* I hoped I wouldn't faint right then and there. I tried my best to think like a hostess and not a slobbering fan. Motioning toward the living-room couch, I said, "Take a seat right here while I go look for her. Can I get you something to drink?"

I noticed that he took a seat exactly where I'd pointed, which showed that he took direction well. He must be an amazing actor to work with. Still smiling, he said, "No, I'm fine." Then he winked at me.

Before I could further ogle him, my mom made her grand entrance.

"Chaynin, how are you? Looks like you're ready to go." My mouth dropped open. She was wearing a white cowl top with an age-inappropriate plunging neckline and dark denim jeans. Not what I was expecting from her on a weeknight. She looked sexy, like, way too sexy.

She beamed at Chay and then gave him a familiar hug and kiss on the cheek as he rose from the couch.

"Wow, you look amazing." He seemed as shocked as I was.

Turning to me, she said, "Chloe, I'll see you tomorrow. Be sure to finish your homework." Gesturing toward the door, she turned to Chay. "Shall we?"

He nodded and dutifully followed her out.

I kept the front door open a little longer, watching as Chay rushed to open the passenger-side Porsche door for my mom. Where was she going with Chay, dressed like that? I wasn't sure, but it didn't seem as if the two of them were headed for an innocent night out on the town. I felt a huge surge of disappointment. Obviously my mom wasn't serious about giving my dad a chance.

The next morning, my tabloid star power grew exponentially. My mom hadn't come home from her date. A little disconcerting, but then again, she was a grown-up—at least most of the time. But then I got a text from Rachelle.

**OMG, Chay Powers!?! How hot was he?**

The word was out. I reluctantly texted her back.

**Yup, superhot.**

On my way to school Vickie texted to tell me to check my e-mail. I ducked into the computer lab on the way to my first class, avoiding all the stares and snickers. With a subject heading of "I think you should know . . ." Vickie had sent me a link to a gossip blog, which I reluctantly clicked on.

And there it was—the feature headline story. A pictorial spread of my mom and Chay's evening (and early morning). A very public dinner at The Ivy. A trendy jaunt to Ritual, a guaranteed go-to-be-seen night club. Pictures of her sitting on his lap, of her dancing on the table, of him looking every inch the new man in her life were splashed on the computer screen before me. I was horrified, mortified, and frankly, nauseous.

"And you didn't even think to call me? Some friend you are!" Rachelle snuck up behind me and jerked the mouse out of my hand. She scrolled through the pictures and sighed. "I wish Chay Powers had come to my house. Even if it was for my mom."

Wide-eyed, she turned to me and grabbed my shoulders. "What if Chay becomes your stepdad? You'll have the hottest dad ever!"

"Rach, what're you talking about? I don't want Chay to be my stepdad. My parents aren't even divorced."

"It would be pretty great, though, right? Chaynin Powers as your dad? I'd totally be over all the time."

"Ugh, I can't deal with this right now. I'll see you later." Trying to put that horrifying thought out of my mind, I grabbed my bag and headed off to class.

"What? Chloe?" Rachelle called after me, but I just kept walking.

It was the longest morning ever as girls I didn't even know nodded knowingly in my direction. I ignored everyone as best I could and tried to lay low.

At lunch I passed up sitting with Rachelle, Joanna, and Ashley and instead hid on a bench with Vickie.

"I couldn't believe those pictures of your mom." Vickie was reacting exactly the opposite of Rachelle and everyone else, which is what I love about Vickie. She was always down-to-earth and able to rationally understand a real crisis. She wasn't excited about Chay Powers at all—even if she agreed he was deliciously hot—but actually articulated exactly what I was worried about. "You must have felt terrible. I would have, seeing my mom out like that." She picked at her salad.

"We had just gone shopping and to brunch, and she had promised she would try talking to my dad, even after his whole stupid stunt. I don't know what she's thinking."

"Are you going to ask her if she's seeing Chay again?"

I laughed. "That's what everyone's been asking me all day."

Vickie cringed. "Sorry."

"No, it's not your fault. I know you're asking because you understand. It totally sucks to see my mom being so, well, obvious and pathetic."

There was really no other way to put it. My mom had decided to fight fire with fire and was probably just trying to make my dad jealous or something. Which in a way was the right thing to do, but, really, how immature. How were my parents going to be civil to each other if they kept on fighting through the tabloids?

Vickie nodded in support. "She seemed like she would be above all that." She paused before continuing. "Sorry if seeing the pictures made your whole day crappy."

"I'm not going to shoot the messenger, Vick." I laughed. "At least I know why everyone was staring at me all day."

"Well if you want to hang out or talk this weekend, I'll be around." Then she quickly added, "I mean, if you don't have anything else to do."

Vickie always did this. Offered to hang out but with disclaimers, as if I always had better options available and she was my last choice. I wondered if that was my fault, if I had given her the impression that I'd rather hang out with Rachelle.

"No, we'll totally hang out this weekend." I assured her. "Thanks."

The bell rang, signaling the end of lunch. As we separated and I headed off to class, I vowed to not take Vickie so much for granted.

As the day went on, I tried to deal with the mixed feelings I had about my mom thrusting herself into dating—all cougarlike, with someone who could feasibly be my older brother—so soon after I had found out about everything. Sure, it had been kind of exciting to have Chaynin Powers show up at the door, but that didn't make up for how inconsiderate she was being. Did she realize how much her actions affected my life at school? The last few days had been spent having to fend off people who just wanted to know about my parents' love lives. Or wanting to make fun of it. I felt like a laughingstock. "Oh look, her parents are divorcing, and look at who they're getting together with instead!" Would every day be like this?

Finally, the last bell of the day rang, and I couldn't get out of Newton fast enough. I booked it to my car and saw Austin waiting for me. Ugh, just who I didn't want to deal with right now. I didn't need any more drama. Then again, he looked really cute leaning casually against my car.

"Somebody forget to call two days ago?" I said as I approached.

He smacked his forehead. "That's right. I guess I just had too much homework on Wednesday." He smiled, and I was sure he was making excuses again; but I wasn't surprised. Austin always had terrible follow-through.

"And yesterday?"

"And yesterday you weren't in school. I figured you were sick or something,"

"If you thought I was sick, why didn't you call to see if I was okay? Or if I needed anything?" This was exactly why we had broken up before. Austin was the poster boy for the out of sight, out of mind mentality.

"Were you sick?" he asked.

"That's not the point, Austin. If we're going to date again you better start paying attention." I couldn't help giving him a flirty pout.

He smiled. "We're going to date again?"

"Maybe, if you shape up," I said coyly. The thought of hanging out with Austin seemed really comforting right now, as if he reminded me of how life was before all of this divorce stuff happened. Plus, he looked extracute today.

"Well, let's start by going to the Lakers game tonight." Austin's dad had a permanent luxury box at the Staples Center. Austin was obviously a huge basketball fan, and I'd learned to appreciate the game with him. This was as good an opportunity as any to rekindle something with him.

"Fine. Pick me up at my house then, and you'd better be on time and on your best behavior," I mock warned.

"Okay, I'll call you." He held up his left hand to his face like a phone and smirked. I hated how cute he could be sometimes.

I practically flew home as I mentally prepared for *my* hot date.

When I got home, my mom was already getting ready for another evening out on the town. I looked at her slinky dress, cut dramatically low and revealing a whole lot of décolletage. I cringed with embarrassment. "Wow, Mom, that's a, umm, pretty serious dress. Who're you going out with?"

"Just Irish," she answered.

"Irish Langdon?" Her recently divorced costar from her most recent romantic drama movie, *Another Night Begins.* The two were rumored to have been involved in an on-set romance years ago, but nothing was ever substantiated. Now those rumors seemed to be frighteningly not too far off base.

Noticing me looking at her disapprovingly, she said, "Yes. We're only friends, Chloe. It's just nice to get out sometimes."

That didn't exactly make me feel any better. It didn't take a genius to figure out what my mom was doing. She was going to out-party my dad, and it looked as if she was on track to make up for lost time. At least Irish was in her age ballpark.

"So, have you talked to Dad yet?" I asked accusingly.

"Not yet," she said. "He left me a few messages, but I'm in no mood to talk to him right now."

It occurred to me that maybe I should call him, but I still

felt loyal to my mom. Plus, this was really something they could handle by themselves, right? I mean, we're all adults here. At least they are. Or at least they should have been.

"Maybe you should talk to him soon."

"Mmhmm," she said dismissively as she fussed with her hair.

Sighing, I gave up. "Okay, well, I'm going to the Lakers game later."

"With Austin?" She raised her voice inquisitively.

I couldn't help smiling. "Yes, with Austin."

"That's fine. Don't stay out too late."

Right back at you, Mom.

Austin picked me up—on time—dressed in a button-down and jeans, and in his dad's silver Maserati. When we arrived at the Staples Center, he surprised me by leading us through a different entrance. "We're not going to your dad's box?"

"Nope, my dad hooked us up with courtside seats. I thought you would enjoy sitting a little closer to the action tonight."

I excitedly grabbed his arm as we headed in. I noticed he kind of limply held on. Still, this was going to be a great night. I could feel it.

Austin wasn't kidding when he said we had courtside seats. We were right on the court near the home team's foul line. Best seats in the house. Seeing a game this up close and personal was amazing, so much better than watching it from the luxury boxes.

At halftime I noticed that Leo and Tobey were a few seats

down from us, and they waved hello. Having a movie star mom did have some perks.

As I took it all in, I noticed that photographers had their cameras trained on me. I cringed, feeling suddenly self-conscious.

"Austin, what's with all the paparazzi?"

"It's just what happens when you sit courtside," he said, leaning back in his chair. He reached over to take my hand, displaying it prominently in his lap.

I smiled and tried to ignore the flashing cameras. I was here to have a good time.

The game was exciting; but during the first few minutes of the third quarter, the Lakers went on a run, and Austin kept hugging me after every big basket. He also latched on to my hand the entire time. I was starting to get suspiciously uncomfortable.

Old doubts came creeping back in my mind as Austin seemed more interested in showing off for the cameras than in watching the game. During a time-out, the huge Jumbotron flashed shots of all the celebrities in attendance; and when they unexpectedly panned over to show us, Austin seized the moment to grab me and stick his tongue down my throat, to the cheers of the crowd.

I pushed him away. "Austin!"

"I couldn't help myself; you just looked so adorable." He winked, more at the camera than at me. The crowd roared its approval. Of course, everyone was now staring at us. I didn't even have to look around to know that we were suddenly the center of attention. Some guy yelled out from behind us, "Do it again!"

Austin looked like he was about to do it when I backed up and shook my finger in his face. "Don't you dare!"

Around us the arena erupted in cheers and catcalls, and I felt the sudden hot flush of being humiliated. Austin was just smiling, soaking in the attention and almost egging them on.

There was no way I was going to stay to finish the game after that. I snatched my purse and jumped out of my seat. Storming toward the exit tunnel, I almost tripped in my haste to leave, and one of the players on the bench actually reached out his hand to steady me.

Austin raced after me as the crowd jeered. "Wait, Chloe! What're you doing?"

"Un-freaking-believable. I can't believe I was dumb enough to think you'd changed. I'm done! It's over, Austin. *O-V-E-R.*" I couldn't believe he'd been so, well, opportunistic when I was at my most vulnerable. Suddenly I saw how stupid I'd been.

"Baby, don't say that. I'm sorry, okay? We were on the Jumbotron. I had to do it."

My jaw dropped in shock. "You're a total jerk." With that I fled toward the exit, desperate to get home. If Austin just wanted to be seen with someone famous hanging off his arm, it wasn't going to be me, not if I could help it. I deserved better.

I grabbed a taxi outside the arena. As we sped away, for some reason I started crying and couldn't stop the whole way home. Was I crying about him? Or maybe it was everything going on in my life. Whatever it was, I was going to need more than a hot bath and a bag of gummy penguins to make me feel better.

# Chapter 5

I awoke the next morning with a massive headache. My life had officially begun a downward spiral—and I'm only sixteen! Let's recap, shall we? Tuesday I found out about the divorce. Wednesday my dad shows up drunk. Thursday my mom goes out dressed like a Hilton; and yesterday, just when I thought things might be getting better, Austin was a total jerk.

I needed some serious chill time, and my tradition of brunch with the girls at The Farm in Beverly Hills on Saturday couldn't have come at a more perfect time.

When I arrived a little after one, Rachelle, Joanna, and Ashley were already seated at a table on the outdoor patio.

"Hi, ladies!" I said, as everyone smiled at me. "Um, let's sit inside. I really don't want to be out in the open like this. I need a paparazzi-free day after the week I've had."

"Oh c'mon, Chloe. It's such a nice day," Rachelle said.

"Nope—not up for discussion. I need peace and quiet."

With a huff, Rachelle and the girls grudgingly got up and moved indoors.

"You know," Rachelle said as we sat down, "it's so fabulous you're in the news every day. I don't even need to call you anymore to know what's going on. It's like I can just pop open the Internet and there you are. For example, what's the deal with you and Austin? I didn't even know you two were back together."

I rolled my eyes. "Ugh. We aren't. You didn't see what happened afterward."

"You got in a big fight?" Ashley and Joanna both chimed in at the same time.

"Of course we did. He was being an attention-grabbing dirtbag."

"Amend that to 'hunky, attention-grabbing dirtbag,' please. That's the headline from the *Gossiper* this morning. They called Austin *hunky*."

"Well, he sort of is if you think about it," Joanna added.

"It was disgusting what an ape he was for the cameras. And the way he rammed his tongue down my throat." I said that last bit a little too loudly, and the couple next to us turned to give me a surprised look. I blushed.

"You are just great at attracting attention lately," Rachelle said, as she flipped open a menu.

"Whatever," I said, rolling my eyes. "Let's order. I'm starving."

When Francisco, our usual server, arrived, Rachelle serenaded him with an affected French accent. "*Garçon*, what can you recommend today?"

"Sorry, Franky, she's in a weird mood," Ashley said. "We'll just have the usuals all around."

Rachelle snapped her menu shut and handed it to Francisco. "Not me. I'll take the Raisin Hazelnut French Toast and a side of granola. *Merci beaucoup.*"

Turning her attention back to me as Francisco left, she said, "Okay, so who's your mom dating next? I've made a list of people I think she should see so, you know, *we* can see them."

"I'd rather she not date anybody. Don't you think it's weird that she's dating so soon?" This was the big thing that was frustrating me. It may have been cool for my friends to ogle my mom's potential suitors, but ultimately it just made me feel as if she was stooping to my dad's level, playing this petty game of trying to out-date him.

"Look, would you really want your mom to take your dad back after what he did?" Rachelle asked. "She's doing the smart thing: making him jealous and moving on. Which is what you should do. Hint, hint."

"You guys are so romantic," I quipped.

"Just pragmatic," Joanna said. "Everyone knows Hollywood marriages don't last. Your parents have been together for, what? Like your whole life? Do you know how weird that is?"

I didn't think that was weird, actually. I mean, they were in love and had made a forever commitment to each other. Wasn't I living proof of that? You don't go out of your way to adopt someone if you don't think you're in it for the long haul.

"If they've been together for so long, you'd think my mom

would make an extra effort to see his side of it. Or maybe he could do something more than show up drunk with a half-assed apology. Doesn't it just make sense that the longer you're together, the harder you'll try to make it work?"

All three of them looked at one another and then at me sympathetically. Joanna even reached out and patted my head. "Chloe, sometimes the longer you're together, the more you need to break up."

"Seriously, you are the cutest thing sometimes," Rachelle said. "At least you had a dad growing up. Some of us weren't that lucky."

I sighed.

"Alright, enough about Chloe. We're going to pop her perfect little bubble world if we keep talking about this. Let's talk about me."

Always leave it to Rachelle to lighten the mood . . . and switch the focus to herself. In this case, I was grateful. Maybe they were right. My parents had stood the test of time in Hollywood marriage years, which had to be similar to dog years or maybe even longer. Regardless, they were my parents, and I didn't want them to split up.

Our food finally came, and the conversation switched to much lighter things. When we were finished, we all decided to see a movie at Grauman's Chinese Theatre.

As we made our way over to the theater a showing had just ended, and people flooded out through the doors. In the crowd, I saw Austin heading toward us. A woman stepped aside to throw something away in a nearby trash can, and I got a good look at who he was with.

Stacey Macedo.

I gasped. Austin had his arm around her waist and was laughing at something she was saying to him. Something idiotic, I was sure.

I stopped in my tracks and grabbed Rachelle by the arm. "We have to go, right now." Without waiting for an answer and hoping that Austin and Stacey hadn't seen me, I turned and dashed around the nearest corner. Just in time too, as Austin and Stacey bumped into Rachelle, Joanna, and Ashley.

"Austin . . . and Stacey? Hello," Rachelle said, trying not to snicker.

The five of them looked confused for a moment as Joanna started looking around for me and Rachelle tried her hardest not to burst out laughing. I noticed that Austin had dropped his arm from around Stacey's waist as quick as he could.

"Uh, hi, Rachelle, ladies."

Rachelle started looking in the direction she'd last seen me but knew better than to call me out.

Stacey, after a few seconds of watching Rachelle, smiled. "Hi, Rachelle," she said, and moved even closer to Austin and grabbed his arm. Her face looked so smug that I was sure she had figured out that I was around somewhere.

After an awkward few minutes of chitchat, Rachelle looked at her watch. "Well, sorry to say hi and run, but we have a movie to catch. See ya."

Stacey and Austin looked relieved as Rachelle and the girls went to the ticket counter. I waited to make sure they were way out of sight before reemerging from my hiding place. I couldn't believe it. Austin and Stacey? Were they in some sort of secret alliance to ruin my life even more?

Rachelle shook her head as I walked up to her.

"Don't say anything. The whole thing is embarrassing."

"Oh, stop. If anything, Austin should be embarrassed he's even touching Stacey. And less than one day after your date."

"Ugh, I know. I don't want to think about it anymore. Let's just watch the movie."

I suffered through a romantic comedy about a girl who loses her boyfriend to a manipulative older woman and then the main character gets to live out the rest of her days in an old house with a dozen cats and a sentient rocking chair.

Okay, fine, that wasn't the movie we watched. But it may as well have been, because that's what I was thinking the whole time, since that would have been the movie Hollywood made about me, Austin, and Stacey.

Ashley and Joanna had to go home after the real movie we watched: a romantic comedy but with a much happier ending than the one I had been envisioning. Rachelle and I headed back to my house to try to figure out why Austin and Stacey were together. Or more importantly, why I even cared.

"See," Rachelle said, as she sat on my floor, only the mildest bit of sympathy in her voice. "If you'd just told me you were still secretly in love with him, I would have warned you off before you went to the Lakers game."

"What? You knew? What about not keeping things from me?"

"I'm sorry. But I didn't know you wanted him back. Plus, they had only gone out on two dates. I didn't think it was serious." Grabbing my hand, Rachelle pulled the pillow off my head and dragged me off the bed. "Listen, I'll make it up to you. C'mon, let's go out. I know just the place. Maison."

I slipped out of Rachelle's grasp and collapsed onto the bed again. "There's no way we're getting in there. And I really don't feel like partying right now."

"You may not feel like it because your whole life is in ruins, but I'm telling you, it's time to move on to something new. And what better way than going out and having an amazing time? C'mon, I have a way to get us in. I know you're just as curious as I am to go!"

She was right of course. It wouldn't do to spend any more time thinking about Austin and Stacey. He could date anybody he wanted as long as it wasn't me. His loss.

"Ugh, fine. But I'm not going to have fun," I said with a smirk.

"Ha, right. You'll have a blast," Rachelle said, already raiding my closet.

After two hours of outfit changing and makeup scheming (and a quick dinner of take-out), Rachelle and I were on our way downtown decked out in matching stilettos. I let her borrow my new flimsy Diane von Furstenberg skirt, which she matched with a backless halter, while I wore denim skinny jeans and a tiered print top. I left a message for my mom and then ordered car service so I wouldn't have to drive.

As we pulled up to Maison at ten o'clock, a large crowd was already gathered outside, and there were lines forming on either side of the entrance. Maison used to be a water treatment facility before it'd been sold and renovated into the newest downtown hot spot. Just last month it had been the site of an Oscars after-party.

"So, how are we getting in?" I asked Rachelle as we stepped out of the car.

Rachelle laughed as if I had just said the funniest thing in the world. "Chloe, *you're* getting us in! You're the belle of the ball right now. They'll be dying to let you into Maison. Trust me."

"Rachelle, after the week I had, you're using me to get into the club?" Sometimes Rachelle just didn't get it.

"Come on, Chloe. You need to have fun, and this is a great way to do it."

I sighed. I guess she was doing it to be nice to me, in a very roundabout way.

Confidently striding up to the bouncer, Rachelle shoved me forward. "This is Chloe-Grace Star, and I'm Rachelle Torres. I believe you know who we are?"

The bouncer gave us the once-over and mumbled, "Not really. Are you on the list?"

*At least one person didn't read the tabloids.*

Rachelle said, "No. We don't have to be."

The bouncer didn't look impressed. "You guys are out past your bedtime. This club is twenty-one and older. Come back in a few years."

"Are you kidding me—," Rachelle said loudly. People in line started to pay attention and began pointing at us, or more accurately, me.

The bouncer noticed the attention. "Hang on a second," he said, and signaled inside for a host to come out.

I recognized the host as soon as he stepped through the door. I'd met him once or twice on occasions when my mom had people over to the house. The overly fake bake hue of his skin and his short, spiky blond hair were pretty memorable. "Hi, Ron."

"Chloe-Grace? What a surprise!" He took an approving glance at our outfits. "You certainly look like you're ready to party. Are your parents with you?" He looked around for a second before he realized what he'd asked. "Ahem, I mean, is your mom or dad here with you?"

"Nope, it's just me and my friend. This is Rachelle Torres."

He looked over at Rachelle, and his face barely registered a flicker of recognition even as he enthusiastically said, "Of course, Rachelle Torres. How are you tonight?"

"I'd be doing a lot better inside, if you please." And then the supersweet smile only Rachelle could pull off.

The host motioned for the bouncer to slide the guard rope aside. "Well, come on in, and I'll take you to the VIP room."

We stepped past the rope—Rachelle giving the bouncer a so-there look—and slipped through the door behind him.

Trendy pop music blasted inside as Ron took us through the art deco-chic club and up a red-carpeted staircase, past plush couches surrounding the dance floor, to the upstairs VIP area, which was outfitted with ultrawhite vinyl couches and a private dance floor and bar. The entire upstairs was empty except for the two of us. As we took a seat, Ron said, "Okay, girls, I'll be right back with something to start you off."

We smiled as he walked away. Rachelle and I moved near the balcony's railing and peered over to people watch. The dance floor was still mostly empty; but there was a trio of girls hanging near its edge, and they started to dance to the music. By the time the three of them made their way to the middle of the dance floor, a group of adventurous guys had already moved in.

Ron returned with two martini glasses filled with premium white grape juice and garnished with a slice of strawberry, and two bottles of water.

Rachelle was about to take a sip of her drink when she paused. "Wait, what're we toasting to?"

I lowered my glass to think for a second. "How about 'out with the old and in with the new'?"

"Sure, sounds righteously messy to me." She raised her glass high, and we clinked to newness.

The faux-tinis were perfectly chilled and silky smooth, and we immediately asked Ron for more. Rachelle looked at him and said, "I'd like mine with a little something extra, please."

Ron winked knowingly. "Got it. Just keep it upstairs, okay? Did you want one of the same, Chloe-Grace?"

I declined politely. As soon as he left, Rachelle excitedly gasped at me. "This is so great going out with you. They'll totally let us do anything!"

I smiled wanly. The club started to heat up by then, and Rachelle and I danced on our balcony as we continued to look over at the crowd.

"Hey! Isn't that DJ Upside?" Rachelle screeched. She pointed at the dj booth. Standing off to one side was a really tall, spindly guy looking slightly bored and entirely out of place in the cosmopolitan crowd with his plain black T-shirt and baseball cap.

"That's totally him." Rachelle grabbed my hand in excitement. "Is he about to start spinning?"

If I didn't know better, I would have said the kid was lost. But I did know better, and this scrawny kid was the youngest person ever to win the Experiments in Sound contest. Rachelle loved his music. I wasn't quite as rapturous and didn't know what the big deal was.

"I'm gonna go talk to him. You wanna come?"

"No, it's okay," I said. "I'll watch from up here."

Rachelle shrugged and headed down the stairs. I took a seat on the nearest couch and let out a breath. The music began to wash over me as I reached for a bottle of water. I just sat back when a gaggle of girls, led by none other than Donna Evans, child star extraordinaire, came shrieking up the stairs.

Donna had her big breakout movie when she was just

fourteen and had garnered critical acclaim for her role as a possessive underage girlfriend. Since then, however, she'd tended to appear in more clubs than movies, and I was hard-pressed to remember her last big role. Tonight she was already well on her way to being trashed as she made a beeline for me.

"Ohmigod! Chloe-Grace! What are you doing here sitting all by yourself, you precious little thing. Where's your mom? We just went out with her yesterday!"

"Really?" I tried to hid my surprise and was a bit taken aback by her enthusiasm. I got up and gave her a quick hug before sitting back down.

She turned to her giggling friends and announced, "We've got to show this girl a good time. Look at her sitting here all alone!" Her friends made fawning sounds, and I was suddenly painfully aware of how young I must have looked to them.

Donna flopped down next to me and looked at me with overdramatic concern plastered on her face. "I feel so bad for you! You must be having the worst time ever with your parents getting divorced."

"Yeah." I wasn't ready to say much more than that. I was still getting used to the idea that my mom had been out clubbing with Donna Evans. Maybe that's how she kept meeting all these young Hollywood guys?

Brightening into a megawatt smile, Donna said, "Well, I'm really glad that you're out and everything. How old are you now?"

"Sixteen," and I added, "but seventeen in May."

She leaned back dramatically into the couch. "Oh, I wish I was

young again. That was so fun. I had the craziest times back then."
She made it sound as if she was past her prime at age twenty-one.
I knew better. Last time I saw her at a club, she had to be car-
ried out by security before midnight. "Listen, forget about your
parents' issues. It's such a downer. Who cares. You're still famous.
Just live it up."

Downing her drink, and with her friends suddenly clustered
back around us, Donna grabbed my arm and dragged me off the
couch. "C'mon, I love this song. Let's go dance!"

Maybe Donna was right. Maybe I just needed to have a little
fun.

I let Donna steer me downstairs to the dance floor. Rachelle
loved this song too, and she was already onstage, dancing in front
of the dj booth. I pointed her out to Donna, and the whole gaggle
of girls hopped up onstage as Rachelle shimmied her way over to
me.

"I totally flirted with Upside," she shouted above the music.
"His real name's Phil, and he said he can get us into all the awesome parties if we just call him. Look." She grinned and showed
me her arm with a phone number scrawled out in black Sharpie.
"We're totally in."

"Great," I said, feigning enthusiasm. As we were grooving and
dancing away, guys were pointing and gawking at Donna, and she
rapturously soaked in the attention. She eventually stepped off
the stage and on to the main dance floor, motioning for all of us
to join her.

Donna started doing exaggerated model poses while she

danced, and people started pulling out their camera-phones and snapping pictures. I really envied Donna. It seemed as if she didn't have a worry in the world. I couldn't remember the last time I felt so carefree, especially with everything that had happened this past week.

At that moment I decided to forget it all—to let it all go and have some fun. I started dancing to the music, letting it wash everything away, and Rachelle looked over and gave me a thumbs-up.

Suddenly, two girls came up to me and screamed, "Hey, can we take a picture with you?"

Ready to give fun a chance, I didn't even hesitate and yelled back, "Sure!" I smiled broadly for the camera and made sure Rachelle was in the picture with me. Even before we were finished, another group of fans accosted me for a picture, and Donna came jumping into the frame at the last second.

By this time, the energy in the club was at fever pitch (turns out DJ Upside was actually pretty good), and we were wildly screaming, taking photos with everyone, and tearing up the dance floor. It felt so good to let loose like this. Rachelle and Donna were new best friends, I was actually having a great time, and I felt as if maybe this was going to be a really memorable night. This was the perfect way to forget about my parental issues. Just pure adrenaline-pumping fun.

After two and a half songs, I motioned to Rachelle and made my way off the dance floor to a long line of girls waiting for the bathroom. I stood patiently while idly people watching. Suddenly, waves of partiers stopped dancing, and an excited murmur broke out. Following their gaze, I looked toward the entrance and saw the one person I least expected to see here: Caroline Treasure.

She was dressed in a very tiny skirt and a really tight halter top, the kind with the middle held together by only a small metal ring. Her gigantic fake boobs looked as if they were about to burst out of their confinement. She had just walked in and was talking and laughing with one of the bouncers.

The girl next in line looked over at me and uttered a low "Whoa."

I couldn't believe that of all the places in L.A., Caroline Treasure would be here. So much for letting loose and having fun. I wanted to scream. Staring at her, I wasn't sure if I wanted to go over and yell at her or to hide so that she'd never see me.

Before I could sort out those options, or even find Rachelle, a hand reached out to grab my shoulder. I flinched and reactively pulled away. Turning around to see who had been so rude, I was given the shock of my life. Standing behind me, with his arm still partly extended from grabbing me, was my dad. This time I screamed a little before it died into a quiet whimper.

"Chloe-Grace, what are you doing here?" My dad's face was flushed with anger.

The shock of seeing Caroline Treasure was intensified now that I understood who she was with. By this time the whole crowd had stopped dancing, and everybody was watching.

I couldn't even speak.

"Forget it; we're leaving." He reached out, firmly grasped my hand, and dragged me toward the entrance.

As we passed Caroline Treasure, she turned to follow us, but he motioned to her and said, "Wait upstairs; I'll be back."

As I was being half dragged outside and across the cement sidewalk, I realized that Rachelle wasn't with me. I finally found my voice. "Dad, Rachelle's still in there. We can't leave without her."

My dad slowed down and looked at me. "Rachelle's here?" Then he looked up into the sky in exasperation. "Of course she is."

Arriving at a waiting limo, he reached for the door and held it open for me to get in. "Max, go get Rachelle." Max, my dad's driver and bodyguard, dutifully turned around and headed back inside.

"Dad, what is going on?"

"That's what you're going to answer for me, young lady. Where's your mother?" He used his body to nudge me into the limo and then shut the door behind us.

Answering his own question, he continued, "Well, she's obviously not here."

I slid all the way to the opposite side door and crossed my arms in front of me.

"Chloe, how much have you been drinking?"

I stared at him defiantly for a second and finally snorted out, "Dad, you know I don't drink."

"Well, I didn't think you went clubbing, either, but here you are."

Looking around the limo cabin, I saw scattered bottles of alcohol and a few half-finished drinks lying around. "That's hilarious. I should be asking *you* how much you had to drink." I knew that was the wrong thing to say, and I didn't really mean it, but it was too late.

"Chloe-Grace! You're sixteen years old, and you're at a club you're way to young to be in. What did you expect me to do? I'm your father!"

I tried to raise my voice above his. "What are you talking about? *Now* you suddenly remember you're my father? You sure haven't been acting like it."

My dad's face totally fell, and he looked as if he'd been punched in the stomach. He stopped yelling. I kept going, though, even as tears welled up in my eyes and I had trouble speaking clearly.

"You cheated on Mom, you showed up totally drunk at the house with an entourage of paparazzi and then got kicked out, and you don't even try to make things right."

I let it all out now—all the frustration I'd been feeling—and threw it all at my dad.

"So I went clubbing tonight without your permission. So what? What're you going to do? Ground me? You don't even live at home anymore. What's Mom going to do? Both of you are out there acting like you're twenty, partying like crazy. What am I supposed to do with that?"

My dad just looked at me and sighed. "Chloe, I'm so sorry." He gathered me in his arms, and I willingly went—feeling like things used to be. "About everything. I just didn't expect to see you out like this." He paused. "And I'm sorry about the other day. I really shouldn't have shown up at the house like that. Even Caroline thought . . . Well, anyway, I'll make it up to you. I promise."

I didn't want him to make it up to me, because everything horrible had already happened. I wanted him to fix everything, for him to come back and explain himself to Mom, and to get back together with her. But I knew deep down that they were way past that, and that crushing realization just made me cry even harder.

A knock on the window interrupted us. "John? I have Rachelle here. Is everything alright?" my dad's driver asked.

I tried to gather myself but couldn't stop sobbing quite yet. "Max, give us a minute."

"Actually, the cameras are starting to get here. We really should go."

My dad looked down at me and asked, very gently, "Chloe, we should probably go. You okay?" Wiping my eyes and taking a deep breath, I nodded yes.

"Alright, Max, let's go." The door opened, and Max helped Rachelle in. She looked at me and my dad, and didn't say a word, which was pretty incredible for Rachelle.

Of course, the silence didn't last long, because even before we pulled ten feet away from Maison, Rachelle looked at my dad and said, "You're, like, the most exciting dad ever." She smiled winningly at him, and magically, my dad smiled back.

I smiled too. Only Rachelle could say something like that and get away with it. I leaned back and closed my eyes. After all the emotional energy had been drained out of me, I was totally exhausted. It had felt good to let everything out; and now, at least, I had talked to my dad. Sort of.

We drove the rest of the way in silence, and after a few minutes we pulled up to Rachelle's house.

"Thanks for the ride, Mr. Star. Chloe, call me tomorrow."

"I will," I replied, as I gave her a hug.

As we left her house, I looked over at my dad. "So, where are we going?"

He motioned for me to come sit next to him. I moved over as he reached into his pocket for a cigarette and rolled down the window. I frowned. "Dad, don't smoke. You know I hate it."

He tossed the cigarette out the window without hesitation. "Look, I'm sorry I overreacted. I know it's been hard for you, okay?" I put my head against his shoulder, and he wrapped his arm around me.

"I know what's happening with me and your mom isn't exactly the easiest thing for you. I'm sorry we haven't been able to keep all this family drama away from you, and I know some of it seems a bit crazy. But understand that we both love you tremendously, and we wouldn't do anything that would hurt you."

"I know."

My dad kissed the top of my head. "And we still worry about you—both your mother and I. I'm sorry about tonight, but you're just too young to be going out to clubs like that."

I sighed. "It wasn't even my idea. Rachelle wanted to take me out because I'd been having such a bad week—with the constant paparazzi, defending myself in school, dealing with Austin and the fact that he's now dating my archenemy. . . . Anyway, I think I just need a quiet night at home."

"That sounds like a pretty good idea," he said, as we pulled up to our house.

My dad got out and held the limo door open for me. I scrambled out and gave him a tight hug. I looked up at him. "Do you want to come in? Maybe stay over? Maybe you can even talk to Mom. . . ."

He smiled weakly. "No, I don't think so. I'm not sure your mother would appreciate it. I have to get back to Maison, anyway. They're paying me to show up there."

I backed up from him and gave him a disapproving look, and said only half kiddingly, "Be good, okay?"

"I'll try," he said, chuckling. He looked at me and smiled. "You're a good girl, Chloe. I love you."

"I love you too, Dad." He gave me a good night kiss, and I headed in, exhausted and burned out.

My iPhone beeped the next day, notifying me of a text message waiting. I groggily looked at the clock. Noon. Ugh. I picked up the phone from my nightstand.

U did it again! C *Entertainment Now!* when u get up. Rach.

I threw the phone back on the night table.

Afraid of what I would see, I flipped to channel thirty-six. "Yesterday, Chloe-Grace and her father were caught by cameras exiting Hollywood's hottest club, Maison, after a night of partying with Dad's new girlfriend, Caroline Treasure."

As the image came into full view, I saw grainy footage of my dad and me standing together. It looked as if we were just chatting by the dance floor, not being surprised by each other outside the bathrooms. Then, as the host kept talking, I saw shots of Rachelle and me dancing, along with separate shots of my dad and Caroline Treasure in the club, looking over the very balcony Rachelle and I had been standing on to start the night. They must have gotten those shots after my dad went back. The way they edited the footage together, it looked as if we'd all been at the club having fun together, which was obviously not true at all.

The voice-over said that the footage had been captured by fellow club goers, and then they showed the pictures of me posing with the girls who had asked for a picture. I sat fully upright in bed when Donna Evans popped up on-screen and screamed about how much fun she'd had introducing me to L.A.'s great nightlife. Just what I needed: Ms. Party Central saying she had a blast clubbing with me. I wanted to cover my head in embarrassment even though there was nobody in the room.

A firm knock on the door pulled my attention away from the report. "Chloe? Are you up? We need to talk." My mom didn't sound happy.

I flicked off the TV and rolled back under the covers. "I'm up. Come in."

It was Sunday morning, and one of the few times I'd seen my mom dressed down recently. Just a simple T-shirt and ruffled skirt, like something any regular old mom would wear. She came in carrying a small tray with a plain bagel, strawberry cream cheese, and a glass of orange juice. "I thought you might be hungry." Setting down the tray on my night table, she sat on the bed. "I heard about your big night."

I hesitantly began, "You saw the footage?"

She nodded expectantly.

"Well, I was really upset by my terrible week, so Rachelle decided we should go out."

My mom's thin lips pulled down into a frown. "Okay, and how did your dad come into the mix?"

I hesitated, and wasn't quite sure how to respond.

"Chloe, sit up and look at me."

I emerged from the covers and sat up, taking a sip of orange juice.

She pushed her hair behind her ears and said, "Listen, I don't really think you should be going out without telling me first. Especially with your father. Now, I know I can't believe anything the tabloids say, so I'll give you a chance to explain."

"Mom, I seriously didn't plan on going out yesterday. I'm sorry I didn't ask you first, but you weren't home. And it's not like I went out with Dad; he just happened to be there. It just got kind of crazy."

"If your dad invited you out, you can tell me."

I pounded the bed sheets in exasperation. "Mom! You know how they always do those things. They edited it to look like we were there together. I swear I wasn't there with Dad. Rachelle and I were there hanging out. Then he came in and dragged us out and took us home. That's it."

I could see a sense of relief come over my mom. "And, trust me, we hardly partied with Dad. If anything, he killed our night when he showed up."

Sounding much less suspicious, my mom said, "Well, if that's the case then that's a different story." Reverting quickly to mom mode, she continued, "You really shouldn't be going out to those kinds of places. You guys are too young."

Tell me about it.

"If you two want, you can go out with me."

Visions of being captured on camera again, this time with my mom, swam before me. One embarrassing clubbing experience with a parent was plenty.

"No, thank you. I'll pass. Dad already lectured me about the evils of going out, anyway. I'll let you two do the partying, and I'll be the responsible one."

"Ha, ha. Very funny." My mom, satisfied with the explanation, was just about to leave the room when she turned around and said, "Oh, actually, David suggested that maybe you should try to stay away from anything public for a while. After this fiasco he's not sure he can do anything to stop the paparazzi, and it might be better for you not to give them anything to plaster all over the place. He even suggested that we have the driver drop you off and pick you up at school. Hank can handle the paparazzi better than you can."

"Seriously? That's so restricting." The idea of not even being able to drive myself anywhere seemed horrific. My celebrity prison was getting more suffocating every day.

"Well, we'll think about it. It seemed kind of drastic to me too. Just try to stay out of trouble."

"You too!" I said to her as she left.

I immediately called Rachelle.

"Where were you this morning? I tried calling you." Her voice came through extraloud and I fumbled the volume down on my phone.

"I was sleeping. Why were you up so early?"

"I had an appointment at the day spa. So, did you see the news?"

"Yeah. My mom was not too happy to see what happened, even after I explained things to her."

"But she was fine afterward?"

"Yeah, sorta."

"Cool, wanna go out again?" Rachelle's tone made it sound more like a statement than a true question, as if she'd already decided what we were doing and she was just asking as a mere formality. "I talked to Donna, and she's going to this great new place, Les Trois. I've never even heard of it before. She says we'll have the time of our lives."

"Um, Rach, I don't think I'm going to go out tonight."

"Seriously? You said you didn't get in trouble, and your mom was fine."

"Hello, did you watch closely? Nothing they reported was even true, I mean, not really."

"Well, whatever, the important part is that now everyone will know that we're out and about. We should be able to get in any-where. I'm superexcited. Pick me up at ten?"

I had to burst her bubble. "Rach, seriously, I'm not going to go out tonight. I don't really feel like it, and I didn't have as much fun in retrospect. Plus, I already told Vickie I'd do something with her tonight."

Rachelle fumbled with her cell, and her voice came over loud and clear. "Chloe, you're not going to go out with me? Who cares about your plans with Vickie? She can come too if she wants, although I'm not sure they'd let her in. But still. I mean, c'mon, there's no way your dad's going to show up again!"

"Nope." I was going to have a quiet night just hanging out and doing nothing. Rachelle could go party with Donna and the rest of Hollywood for all I cared. I wasn't up for it at all—if ever. "Seriously, Rach, just go and have fun. I'm sure I'll hear all about it tomorrow."

"Ugh, fine. But you're going to be superjealous when I tell you all about it!"

Jealous of going out and getting thrown on TV with your dad and your dad's girlfriend who just happens to be the reason your parents are divorcing? My eyes had a better chance of melting out of their sockets than turning green with envy.

# Chapter
## 6

With Rachelle determined to go out again, I took the chance to go over to Vickie's for a lazy Sunday evening. She'd consistently offered to have me over to watch movies and just hang out, but I usually had something else to do. I felt bad always putting her on my social back burner, but tonight I needed some serious therapy time, and Vickie was the perfect friend to help.

When I arrived at her house, Vickie already had popcorn, chips, dip, a selection of candies, and two Jamba Juices set out.

"Wow, movie night with you is serious business. I love it!"

"I didn't know what drink you felt like, so just pick one and I'll take the other." This is how Vickie always was, careful to make sure I was comfortable.

"Let's just share both," I answered.

Settling down on the floor, she popped in *Clueless* as background noise, lowering the volume so we could still talk. I quickly filled her in on what had happened the night before with my dad and this morning with the news.

"Ohmigosh. That sounds horrific. Is that why you didn't want to go out tonight?"

I paused to think about it for a minute. "It just feels like every time I go somewhere, something horrible happens. I'd just rather avoid it."

"But Rachelle wanted you to go out with her."

"Yeah, but I don't think she understands how much it sucks when things happen. She doesn't really get weirded out by the attention."

Vickie laughed. "That's an understatement. Well, tonight's not going to be nearly as exciting, I'm afraid."

"That's exactly what I need—a complete change of pace. Plus, we never get to, you know, just hang out."

"So, how was seeing your dad? I mean, you haven't seen him since the whole thing that happened at your house, right?"

"It sucked. I mean, did you watch the news?"

She nodded, almost apologetically. "Yeah. It looked . . . uncomfortable."

"Every time I see him there're cameras all over the place. It's just frustrating. My mom told me that I shouldn't talk to him until she did, but then she's not even making an effort."

"Maybe if you want to talk to him you should just call him? He is your dad, after all."

"Well, we kind of got to talk a little bit in the car after he calmed down. It just made me feel worse, though, because he went right back to the club. And this morning my mom flipped out because, after seeing the news, she thought I had planned to go to Maison with him. She would be really hurt if I did contact him by myself." I paused. "The whole thing is a mess. I'm just so tired of all the drama. Normal kids don't have to worry about getting every detail of their life broadcasted."

"That's true. If you're wondering what regular kids have to go through, just ask me. I'm an expert."

Yeah, I guess she was. Like, this was something I'd always wondered about Vickie: how in the world she seemed to remain so endearingly normal at Celebrity High. It's not as if she was from a different background than I was. Her parents are rich too, and her mom used to be pretty famous. But it seemed as if she has entirely different interests than anybody else I know.

"So…" I wanted to phrase this carefully. "Do you, I mean, do you like being kind of, you know, anonymous?" That's not the exact word I was looking for, but it would have to do.

"You mean do I like not having anyone pay attention to what I do? And people not knowing who I am?"

"Yeah, I guess . . ."

She smiled. "It's got its perks, and it's got its bad parts. Put it this way: I'm glad I don't have to go through what you do all the time. Your life just seems crazy complicated. And not even just now. You had all that drama with Austin recently. . . ."

"Which is still going on. I just saw him with Stacey, of all people."

"Ugh, I don't know how you do it. It would make me absolutely insane dealing with all the things that happen to you."

Vickie was saying this almost in admiration, as if she thought I was a strong person for having a crazy life or something. I knew she was giving me words of encouragement, but I didn't feel strong at all. Just overwhelmed.

I took a deep breath. "You know, sometimes I try to imagine what it would have been like to have been adopted by a normal couple. Not famous at all, but just a perfectly normal family somewhere in Kansas or something. I feel like sometimes I didn't get to make any choices at all."

Vickie frowned. "Well, it's not like you don't get to make any choices. You still decide who you are and what you like to do. It's not something where by being famous you're forced into everything."

She was right, of course, but it's not easy when there are expectations of you from the world. It's not like normal kids have their lives fully documented by millions of strangers. They get room to grow, to make mistakes, to find out what they're all about without everyone watching all the time. I feel like I never got to discover who I really am. I already had to fit a mold.

I looked over at Vickie, who was waiting for me to say something. I reached over to give her a hug. "You're a really good friend, Vickie."

"I know. We anonymous types usually are."

I returned home that night feeling empowered and nostalgic at the same time. All of this got me thinking about who I really am, where I really came from. I mean, I was adopted, so a part of me was left in China. Maybe that part is the real me—the "normal" me? Who am I without the "famous" part?

I went to the trophy room and dug into the pile of magazines and news clippings that dated back to my adoption. Instead of looking at the familiar faces of my Hollywood parents in the foreground of my adoption pictures, I found myself scouring the backgrounds of the photos. I tried to look at the blurry images and edges of the pictures to get an idea of where I had come from. In some of the photos, storefronts and signs were visible, but I didn't have any idea what they said. The most familiar part of the photos to me was my parents, who were foreigners in the pictures. That's weird, right?

Sifting and scanning through the magazine clips and articles, I realized that there was not one mention of which part of China I'd been adopted from. From such a huge place, I didn't have a clue where exactly I had lived, even briefly. It's like they say, you should never forget where you came from; but I didn't even know where I came from. Not that where I was made much sense either, right now.

I'd never told anyone this, but I've thought about my birth parents from time to time. I've wondered if they know what kind of life I've had apart from them. Would they have any idea that their daughter ended up in Hollywood? Did I look like my mom or my dad? Was I their first child, or was I just a girl when they had really wanted a son? Did they have any other children? Were they still in China? Not one magazine clip, photo, or article even mentioned them. It felt really empty not knowing anything about them. And while I had thought about them before, it had never occurred to me that I might never know who I was unless I knew about them. Could eleven months make such a difference? I think it could. After all, I needed to know where I'd been to know where to go, right?

I scanned the articles, looking for signs of who my real parents were. But as I started to clean up the mess I'd made, it occurred to me that it was strange my parents never adopted again. Many of the other celebrity parents who'd adopted kept right on adopting. Some of them assembled an international family of adoptees as they flew around the world plucking children from their home countries and into bigger, grander, and presumably better lives.

Maybe my parents had decided that parenting just wasn't their thing after their experience with me. I kind of wished they had adopted some more, or had kids of their own. Then I would have someone to at least share the spotlight with. As great as Rachelle and Vickie are, I don't think either of them could ever completely understand where I came from or what I had to deal with.

As I left, I took a moment to look again at the framed picture of me, eleven months old, wrapped lovingly in the arms of my ultrafamous mother. I couldn't help wondering, if I'd had the choice, would I have preferred to stay with my birth family, even if that meant being a totally different person? I mean, I would have been a totally different person, right? Nurture versus nature.

Would I trade in being the adopted kid of John Michael Star and Dominique Benjamin just to have a happily normal and regular life instead of this crazy one?

At school on Monday, Rachelle came running up to my locker.

"Ohmigod, Chloe! I have *got* to tell you all about last night at Les Trois!"

"Good morning to you, too," I said, grinning.

"Let me just tell you that we *have* to go back there. Right when I showed up they knew exactly who I was and gave me the full VIP treatment. I really think our night at Maison got us known, you know? Like, really known!"

She was conveniently leaving out the fact that we were already known, and Maison had inched us toward infamy, if anything.

"My night with Vickie was pretty fun too," I began, trying to steer the conversation in another direction.

"Really? What did you guys do?"

"We watched a movie and—"

"Oh! Speaking of movies, can I just tell you that Les Trois was projecting one of your mom's movies on this supergiant screen hanging over the dance floor? I was going to take a video of it for you, but my phone battery was low. I'm not sure which one it was. They all seem kind of the same."

"Speaking of my mom, Vickie and I got to talking about my parents and being famous. It was really interesting. She gave me some perspective on all the craziness that's been going on." I could feel her attention span fading away even as I got more serious.

"That sounds like it was fun. Like a really good change of pace. But seriously, next time you need to come out, okay?"

While I usually loved Rachelle's unbridled enthusiasm about stuff, she was way too hyper and excited for me right now. I didn't want to talk about clubbing when I had so much else on my mind. "Sure," I said, closing my locker. "I'll see you later. I gotta get to class."

"Okay, but let's talk about going out on Thursday night."

I waved dismissively as I made my way down the hall. I felt as if I was going through something and I just needed someone to listen. Rachelle obviously wasn't that person right now.

Near the end of the day I finally got a chance to see Vickie and dragged her inside the nearest empty room to escape the din of the hallways. "You totally inspired me yesterday. I think I want to look for my birth parents." I stood there and smiled as if I'd just made the biggest confession of all time. I waited for her to cheer or something.

When she was a little slow to respond, I quickly added, "So, what do you think?"

"I inspired you?" Vickie's confused reaction wasn't quite what I expected.

"Look, all that talk about being normal and, you know, being able to choose—all that stuff. It just made me think. And I realized something yesterday after I got home. Like, what if I didn't get to choose because I was adopted into this crazy life?"

"I'm not sure I'm following." Vickie looked concerned. "And you're talking really fast so, seriously, slow down."

I took a deep breath before launching into an explanation. "Okay, you know how yesterday you were saying that everyone decides who they are and what they get to do? Like, you know, total free will."

"I'm not sure I said free will exactly," Vickie interjected, "but, okay, go on."

"Okay, fine, probably not your exact words; but that's what I took out of it. So, that idea of being able to choose got me thinking that maybe my choices were totally taken away because I was adopted."

Vickie said cautiously, "So you're thinking you didn't want to be adopted? You don't like your life?"

"No, I do. I mean, normally I do. It just kind of sucks right now. Okay, sucks a lot. And it's not like I don't appreciate being adopted, especially by famous people. But maybe there's something in knowing what my other life might have been like. Basically, I think I want to know what my real parents are like."

"Like, your birth parents?"

"Yeah."

"Aren't they in China?" Vickie was being painfully rational and down-to-earth about this. It felt as if I was doing something big, and I didn't want anyone to tell me differently. After the conversation with Rachelle, I'd decided not to tell her about it because she had a tendency to make things seem unimportant if they didn't relate to her. I wanted this to be important because it felt so big. And I thought Vickie would appreciate the magnitude of my epiphany.

I kept on clasping and reclasping my hands, getting more agitated by the second.

"Okay, okay, Chloe, I got it. You want to figure out who your birth parents are. That's fabulous. Why don't you just ask your mom and dad?"

"That's the obvious solution, of course. I mean, I thought about that, but I'm afraid they would give me some sanitized version of the story and not tell me everything I wanted to know. Plus, I feel like, with this whole divorce thing, the timing is all wrong; and things are so bad between them already. I don't want it to seem like I'm looking for my birth parents because they're fighting."

"Um, isn't that what you're doing?" Vickie pointed out.

Okay, yeah, this was probably exactly what I was doing; but it felt right, even if there wasn't all this divorce stuff going on. I had convinced myself that my motivation wasn't purely about my celebrity parents fighting. I just wanted to find some answers.

"It feels like something I just want to do for myself. You know?"

My eyes must have seemed as if they were pleading, because without hesitating, Vickie nodded. "Sure, of course. So, what are you going to do?"

I was much calmer now that Vickie had voiced her support. I

didn't realize how desperate for affirmation I was that this was the right thing to pursue. It was such a relief, and I felt a sense of ultimate solidarity with Vickie. Not that I doubted her, of course.

"So, I looked through some stuff in the trophy room, but I didn't find much. I didn't find anything useful, actually. All I have is my Chinese name—Shao-Chi—and some pictures."

Vickie frowned. "That's not going to make things any easier. Do you have access to any documents or anything? Like, I dunno, a birth certificate? Passport? Oh, wait, that's not going to help. Well, maybe the birth certificate if you can get it."

"I don't think I can get it. I mean, what would I say? 'Hi Mom, can I see my birth certificate real quick?'" We both smiled. "Not telling my parents isn't going to make this easy, I know."

My emotional high about finding my birth parents was quickly giving way to the logical thought process of exactly how that was going to happen. It had sounded like such a good plan yesterday.

"Well, nobody said doing things your way was ever easy," Vickie teased. "Maybe you should think about some professional help? I mean, I don't really know the first thing about adoptions."

"Do you have anyone in mind?" I asked hopefully.

"Um, nope. But we can ask around, I'm sure. Maybe my parents know somebody."

"Ooh." In another flash of inspiration, it suddenly occurred to me who would be absolutely perfect in this situation. "Actually, I think I know just the person to talk to. Cross your fingers."

\*    \*    \*

After school, wearing dark sunglasses to hopefully avoid any paparazzi—and the wrath of Mom's publicist—I headed over to Cartier, where Jean-Paul greeted me with a robust "*Bonjour, mademoiselle*, it's been too long." He lowered into a dramatic bow and moved to pretend to lock the door behind me. He winked. "Anybody chasing you this time?"

"More than ever." I smiled.

"Well then, Chloe-Grace, how can I be of assistance? Another bracelet? A necklace perhaps?" He moved behind one of the display cases and took out a tray of spectacular dangly earrings in various shapes and sizes.

I wasn't technically here to shop, but they looked irresistible.

Carefully removing a dazzling pair from the tray, he held them up to the light. "Care to try?"

What's a girl to do, right? I slipped them on and admired the look in the mirror. "Actually, Jean-Paul, I was hoping to take you out for coffee, if you aren't terribly busy. I have something to talk to you about."

He theatrically narrowed his eyes and gave me the once-over. "A beautiful girl doesn't mysteriously ask me out to coffee every day. How can I refuse?"

I carefully handed him the earrings. "Can you go right now?"

"With pleasure, *mademoiselle*." He turned to a young woman and said, "Cindy, I'll be stepping out for a bit with Chloe-Grace. Watch the shop while I'm gone."

As we headed out the door, I said a bit apologetically, "Sorry for taking you away from work. I know you're, like, in charge of everything."

"Oh, please, if they can't handle the store without me for a while then I haven't trained them well enough."

We settled down at an outdoor table at La Patisserie, a French bakery around the corner. Once we ordered two cups of café au lait, he crossed his legs and put his hands on his knees in anticipation. "So, what's going on?"

I started slow. "Okay, so you know about my parents, of course."

He grimaced and shook his head in disappointment. "*Oui*, a terrible tragedy."

"And you kind of know what's been going on since then, right?"

"Certainly."

"So"—I steadied myself to collect my thoughts before beginning—"everything's kind of been a huge mess, and I've been having a really hard time at home and school and, well, with just everything."

Jean-Paul nodded sympathetically. "I know. I've seen the tabloids. I'm so sorry."

"Well, with all this family drama going on, I've been thinking about my life a lot; how it could have been different. I need a change."

"Not something jewelry can fix, eh?"

I smiled. "Not this time." I loved how Jean-Paul could show his concern in a funny yet caring way. "I know we've always kind of said that we feel like two of a kind because we're both adopted, right? And recently I've been thinking about that a lot. Well, recently meaning since yesterday." I couldn't believe it'd only been such a short time. Like this revelation about finding my parents had been sitting in me forever even if it was just last night that Vickie had helped to trigger it.

"What I'm saying is that I think I want to find my birth parents. Like how you found yours. I thought maybe you would know something about how to do that." I knew that Jean-Paul had found his birth parents a long time ago, but I didn't know the whole story.

He produced a lighter and delicately plucked a cigarette from his suit pocket. I nodded for him to go ahead. I hated the smell, but for Jean-Paul I'd put up with it.

"My experience wasn't exactly positive. Not that I'm saying you shouldn't look for them, of course." He paused as the waiter set our coffees in front of us. "Anyway, when I was slightly older than you, I was convinced that I had to find my birth parents. I had built up this fantastic idea of a happy reunion and parents who would be delighted to see me. To put it succinctly, they weren't."

As he said this, it highlighted that that's exactly what I'd been thinking. It had never even occurred to me that my birth parents wouldn't be happy to be found. What if they hadn't put me up for adoption out of necessity but because they wanted to?

He took a long drag on his cigarette. "You know, Chloe, sometimes it's better not to go looking for something. Do you understand?" All traces of his normal jovial tone were gone.

I sighed and cupped my coffee mug. "You know what happened when I found my birth parents?" he went on. "I found out they were never married, or even in love. I was sent away for adoption because of it."

This was the first time Jean-Paul had shared that information with me. I knew he was only trying to help, but a wave of sadness washed over me, and it dampened my enthusiasm and put it in perspective. I hadn't really considered that maybe I wasn't the product of another set of parents but of two completely separate people.

I looked up, and JP forced a wan smile on his face."*C'est la vie*," he said, making a flourish with his hand. He crushed his cigarette and threw it into the ashtray in the middle of the table.

"Look, I'm telling you this not to discourage you, Chloe. Not at all. But I just want you to be prepared not to expect a fairy tale. What is it that you're hoping to find out?"

"I think I'm just interested in knowing who they are. Like, they gave birth to me and they're a part of my story, and I'm part of theirs. And maybe that will tell me something about myself."

"So, it's about finding out your history and theirs? It's not about feeling unloved?" He looked at me carefully. "Because that's what I felt. My adoptive family didn't turn out to be so loving and accepting of, well, my lifestyle. I had dreams that my real parents would."

"What do you mean 'about feeling unloved'?"

"Allow me to take a guess and say that maybe you're feeling a bit unloved because your parents are divorcing. But I know your mother and father, and I know that they love you."

"It's not about that. I know they love me." Even as I said it, I knew that this was part of what I was feeling: a bit unloved by my parents. But in the same instant I knew that they did love me, because in all this talk about choice and choosing, I had left out the fact that they had chosen me to be part of their lives, even if it was mind-bogglingly crazy at times.

Jean-Paul brightened and pulled out his smile again. "Then if it's about finding out more about your story, I just want to make sure that your expectations are tempered by whatever reality you'll find. And I'm glad to offer you any help you might need."

"How can you help?"

"Don't worry about that. I know people."

Hearing him say this after revealing his own story to me, I started to cry. It took Jean-Paul three napkins to wipe away my tears, and he gave me a hug.

After I regained some composure, I asked him, "Would you do it all over again? Even knowing how it turned out?"

"I don't live with regrets, Chloe. There's no going back. There's no refund policy on knowledge or life." He added brightly, "That's why I prefer working with things bright, shiny, and fabulously platinum."

We finished our coffees, and I left Jean-Paul with the little information I had gathered. Sadly, I didn't know much of anything except how old I was, when I was adopted (both taken from magazine reports), and my Chinese name. Jean-Paul said he would see what he could do. He promised to contact me as soon as he heard anything.

\*     \*     \*

I had hoped that the new week would wash away all the drama of last week. I had made it through one day without being harassed; and with Jean-Paul helping me out, I thought I would have a chance to find some answers.

Of course, having your parents in the news constantly isn't something that you can just close your eyes to and have go away. My wishful thinking was quickly deflated Tuesday afternoon. I opened the door to my locker and found pieces of paper fluttering out. I managed to snatch one midair before it landed.

I almost wished I hadn't. It was a picture from my night at Maison, obviously printed out from the Internet. A Post-It note stuck in the upper right-hand corner teased, CHLOE, CAN YOU SIGN THIS FOR ME?

My stomach clenched as I felt incredibly violated. It was one thing to talk about me, but to shove this stuff into my personal space like this? That was just so low. Anonymously no less. Actually, this wasn't anonymous; it had Stacey's signature plastered all over it. There was no way I was going to let her get away with this. I picked up the rest of the papers and shoved them in the trash.

Stomping over to Stacey's locker, I seethed and waited. It didn't take long before her obnoxious, lilting voice preceded her and she trotted into view. She was flanked by Heather and Nicole, her usual cronies. Noticing me giving Stacey my best death glare, they stopped talking and slowed down before Stacey grinned and made her way toward me. While I was still definitely fuming, I realized that I was seriously outnumbered and wished I'd had the presence of mind to have at least waited until Rachelle was around.

"Well, well, if it isn't Caroline Treasure's soon-to-be step-daughter. Will she be hyphenating her name?" Nicole and Heather tittered beside her right on cue.

I had to hand it to her; Stacey was nasty and hadn't missed a beat despite being surprised. I should have thought of something to say before she showed up. Instead, I just shoved the picture in front of her so she could read the note.

"You are such a bi—"

The rest of what I had to say was cut off by Stacey's sudden explosion of laughter.

"This is so funny! Pure genius! I wish I had thought of this." She continued to chortle, and I was left trying to decide if she actually had amazing acting skills I wasn't aware of. There was no way she was faking this.

The angry flush faded from my face, replaced by humiliation. "You didn't stuff this in my locker?"

"Oh no, but I wish I had! Nic, look at this!"

I snatched the paper back before she had a chance to show her friends. "This is the funniest thing I've ever seen. Oh God, can I get your autograph, Chloe? Can I, can I?"

"Go to hell, Stacey."

I turned around and stomped away, but not before she managed to get out, "I don't need your autograph; I have your boyfriend!" That stung, and flashbacks of seeing them walk out of the movie together made me want to throw up.

When I finally found Rachelle after school, I wasn't even sure what I was more upset about: the fact that somebody other than Stacey was out to destroy me, or that Austin and Stacey were really together.

"Listen, let's go down to Robertson Boulevard and clean out a few boutiques. You'll feel better." This was Rachelle's way of comforting me. Shopping was our cure-all. But I couldn't even do that.

"I can't go shopping. The cameras are following me everywhere, and I'm supposed to avoid public places if I can."

"You're grounded?" Rachelle sounded as if she'd been the one told not to go anywhere. She swung her locker closed with a loud thud.

"I mean, I'm not grounded or anything." I don't think either of us had been grounded since middle school. "But to be honest, it makes sense not to be out so much when I'm constantly being watched. It's, um, prudent."

"You sound like David now. It's 'prudent'! How are we going to hang out if you can't go anywhere?"

"We can still hang out. Just inside." That sounded lame, and Rachelle was quick to point that out.

"Inside? You mean at home? You don't want to go out at night. You can't go out during the day. What are you planning to do? Just go to school and never do anything else?" Rachelle's eyes widened in exasperation. "One day you're going to realize all this attention's a good thing. People actually pay good money for this kind of attention. There's like a whole industry built around it. Hello."

"Well, it's not like you can't go out. Just me. And we can hang out at other places, just not on Robertson, where people would expect to see us."

"That's just ridiculous. So, pretty much you're saying you can't hang out anywhere cool." Rachelle rolled her eyes. "Fine, I'll just do your shopping for you. And I'll take pictures and send them to you as I'm looking so you can tell me if you think it's cute or not."

That was Rachelle's way of showing she cared for me: the gift of shopping for me and not just for her. It really was Rachelle's highest form of sacrifice. Gotta love her. Unfortunately, that didn't solve my problem. And at this point it seemed as if only hiding from everyone could give me any sort of peace and quiet.

# Chapter

## 7

On Thursday I was summoned back to Cartier with the promise of information. This time Vickie was in tow, to give me moral support. Jean-Paul gave me a warm greeting and then ceremoniously handed me a bulging sealed envelope. "A present."

I didn't waste any time ripping open the envelope and splaying the contents on the jewelry case in front of me.

There was a Chinese newspaper, the text of which had been translated; a small stack of photocopied magazine articles and clips about my celebrity parents; a stack of official-looking papers; and a note written on a slip of paper that read "Call me. Casey."

"Whoops, that's for me." Jean-Paul smiled, and reached over and took the slip of paper.

"How did you get this, and so fast? And who's Casey?"

"Let's just say you should be glad I know so many people. And that I've had my share of failed, but ultimately happy, relationships," Jean-Paul said coyly.

"Ohmigosh, you got this from someone you dated?" I playfully slapped him on the arm.

"Casey is an ex, yes. And he just happens to work at an adoption agency, and I made him make it high priority. And just so you know, this wasn't the most legal of endeavors, so don't go spreading the word on how I got this."

"You seriously have all the connections. I hope it wasn't too difficult." Everything seemed to be falling into place. Surely this was a sign that I was doing the right thing.

"Actually, he said that having famous parents helped your cause tremendously. Sometimes this type of information can take months to get. Having your parents' every move tracked since forever made it a lot easier to find this stuff."

"If it's so easy, I'm surprised the tabloids haven't run this," I said, turning my attention to reading the translated Chinese newspaper. It revealed that my biological parents—the Yuens—had known exactly who adopted me. The article was an exclusive interview with a Szechuan couple who had their daughter adopted by American celebrities. My biological mother was quoted as saying, "We immediately knew who had adopted her because we saw a picture of that famous actress holding her coming off the plane."

This was stunning. Not only would they have known who had adopted me, they would have always known afterward exactly who I was. If they had wanted to, they could have contacted me at any time. The question was, why did they never even try to establish contact in all this time?

Tears—half angry, half sad—welled up in my eyes. Maybe they didn't want to know any more about me. I took a shaky breath and forced myself to keep reading. My parents then said that they were just so happy that their daughter had been given such a luxurious life in America. The interviewer had actually asked them the exact question I'd just asked myself. If they had wanted to contact me.

Their answer was that, to them, they were too poor and couldn't possibly have offered the life I had now, so it was more important that they knew I was healthy and happy. They didn't think of it so much as having given me away as being blessed to have a lost daughter taken into a heaven of sorts. That was enough for them.

Vickie and Jean-Paul were sifting through the other documents, but I could see that they were watching me. "Are you okay?" Vickie asked, concerned.

I nodded as Jean-Paul produced a box of tissues and slid it over to me. All I felt now was an outpouring of relief that it wasn't that they hadn't wanted to contact me but that they'd felt as if I was in a better place.

As I got to the end of the article, my tears were replaced by an icy blast of shock. The last line read "Mr. and Mrs. Yuen will realize their dream of moving to Los Angeles with the proceeds they will earn from this interview. We wish them good luck."

I couldn't even talk. I was shaking so badly, I dropped to the floor and leaned up against the jewelry case to steady myself.

Vickie reached over and gently took the article out of my hands. As she read it and got to the end, she let out a little gasp of astonishment.

"They live here?"

Reacting to both of our stunned silences, Jean-Paul reached over to take the article and read it quickly. "Oh, *mon Dieu*! That's amazing!" he said in a hushed tone.

By this time I was sifting through the rest of the papers and found what I was looking for. I turned the sheet over to Vickie and said, "Look at the address."

"No way! They live in Alhambra? That's near here."

"I know. But it doesn't say how long they've been there."

Jean-Paul said, "Casey assures me that the information in there is recent and accurate."

Suddenly realizing that this meant someone else knew I was looking for my birth parents, I looked at Jean-Paul in panic. "Wait, Casey wouldn't tell anyone about me looking for my birth parents, right? He won't go to the tabloids or anything?"

"Not if he wants me to call him back," Jean-Paul huffed. Knowing that even friends, or exes, sometimes can't resist selling a juicy story, I had my doubts. Seeing my unconvinced reaction, he said, "Don't worry, Casey can be very discreet. It's part of his job. Plus, he isn't starstruck like others. He couldn't care less."

Before I could continue worrying, Vickie let out a small shriek.

Jean-Paul and I both looked at her.

"Chloe, it says here you have a brother." Vickie looked at me wide-eyed, awaiting my reaction.

"What are you talking about?" I grabbed the paper and carefully read about my brother. My little brother!

"Vickie, check this out. Hong-Yin Yuen. He's a freshman at Hollis High. And they have his blog address." I showed her the little section where they had listed some detailed information about my brother.

Everything was suddenly so overwhelming. I turned to Jean-Paul, and warm tears came to my eyes. "I can't even begin to tell you how much I owe you." I couldn't hold it in anymore and broke down, but in the happiest way possible.

"Chloe, you don't owe me anything." He came around and gave me a big hug.

"I'm so sorry," I said, wiping at my eyes. "I totally ruined your suit." Dark wet splotches stained the shoulder and chest area of Jean-Paul's almost certainly very expensive suit.

"Oh please, I should frame this for posterity. Don't even worry about it. This is the greatest day in your life. What's a little moisture?"

After I'd sufficiently gathered myself together, I thanked JP again, and he and Vickie helped me put all the papers back into the envelope.

I dropped Vickie off at her house with the promise to call her. When I got home, I dug everything out and read through it all again.

Before the evening ended I hopped online and read through every word on my brother's blog, carefully picking apart every paragraph, following every link, and completely absorbing everything he'd written or done during the past two years.

I hoped to find pictures of our parents, but he didn't post any photos online. I searched for "Hong-Yin Yuen" on MySpace and Facebook, but both of his profiles were set to private, and messaging him wasn't an option. I mean, how would I explain who I was? "Hi, this is your long-lost sister, let's be friends." Somehow, I didn't think it would go over well.

After a few hours of intense reading, I still felt as if my brother was a stranger. I knew he wasn't big into sports, he was huge into videogames, and his favorite movies were *Armageddon* and, surprisingly, *Serendipity*. That might be one of the few things we had in common. But I was hoping for something that screamed out that we were really, truly related. I'm not sure what I expected to have in common with a boy two years younger than me, but I guess *Serendipity* would have to be it. I was sure there had to be more.

I wanted to meet him. I imagined him writing on his blog about his sister, the one he's been wondering about all these years. He would be amazed to hear about how life had turned out for her, and we could exchange stories about how our parents were.

Mine, famous and on the path to divorce; his (ours), possibly strict and unyielding. Or maybe they were totally relaxed and let him do whatever he wanted. I don't know, but we could compare and contrast once we got to know each other. But then I imagined the press writing about it. And then television crews trying to get my birth parents to agree to an exclusive interview, which would happen, of course.

Some stupid talking head would want to get all over the story. There's no way I could allow that. I didn't want this new part of me to be another piece of media gossip. It felt too important for that. This was mine.

Plus, you can't just thrust your celebrity life into someone else's world, not if they had a choice in the matter. I desperately wanted to meet my brother, to meet my birth parents; but I didn't want to bring the red carpet with me.

There was only one solution. There was only one way I would be able to meet my family. I would have to do it without anyone knowing.

By the next morning I had an entirely bigger plan, one I was trying to outline to my mother as she sat wearily at the kitchen counter across from me. "Chloe, can we talk about this later? I had a late night, and I can't concentrate right now."

I wasn't going to give in this easily. I was on a mission. "Mom, no, just listen. I think I need to get out for a while."

My mom reached for the pot of coffee. "That's fine. Take the day off if you want. You know you don't have to ask me." She moved very slowly and deliberately as she poured herself another cup.

"Not necessarily just today. I was thinking longer."

"The rest of the week?"

"It's Friday, Mom. The week's over." I knew she'd been going out every night this week—everyone knew, actually—but losing track of what day it was spoke volumes about her state of mind.

"I was thinking of transferring. Like going to another school."

My mom narrowed her eyes and looked at me in confusion. "You want to transfer? Is something going on with school?"

"Not with school in general. Just this school. I want to get out of Newton."

"What's wrong with Newton?"

"What isn't wrong with it? Everyone asks me questions every day about you and Dad. Rachelle is going attention crazy. Everything is just getting to be too much. It's really affecting my education." That last part I threw in for effect.

"So, transferring to another school will help? It could make things worse. Have you thought about that?"

Perfect, a direct lead-in to the crux of my plan. "Well, it's not just transferring I want to do. I was thinking I could go to another school—a normal school—anonymously, like not as me. Kind of like in that one movie you did with Deanna Bernstein. You know? The one where she's a reporter who pretends she's in high school in order to get the scoop?"

My mom looked pretty awake after I said this. "If you want to be out of school to avoid everyone there, then we'll just go ahead and take you out of school. I'll hire a couple of tutors, and you can finish the year at home. There's no need for you to go to another school. And to disguise yourself. That just sounds silly."

"It's not a disguise, really. Just, you know, I thought it would be nice if nobody knew who I was. I've never had that before, you know?"

My mom looked at me quizzically. "Do you really think it would make that much of a difference?"

"Yes! You even said it yourself so many times. 'Things are different when nobody knows who you are.'"

My mom laughed. "I meant that the other way—as in things would be bad. Not like what you're saying." My mom's worked so hard to be famous that she can't fathom anyone not wanting to be famous. "Why would you want to be anonymous, Chloe?" Even as she said this, I could sense that understanding was starting to seep in with the caffeine. "So, you want to go somewhere anonymously, where nobody knows you?" She paused and refilled her coffee cup. Sometimes I think my mom took such long pauses in conversations because she was used to rehearsing lines over and over in her head. I'd learned to just stop talking and let her have her quiet moments. But this time I was getting a little nervous. I hoped that I wouldn't have to tell her about my newfound family. That was my final ace in the hole, but I didn't want to use it if I didn't have to. After all, telling her that I wanted to transfer to find my birth family might set off all sorts of alarms for her. And it was true that I really did want to be anonymous, even if part of the motivation was to befriend my brother and to see my family. I thought that my mom would be able to relate more to my wanting to disappear than to my dropping this whole family thing in her lap right away. With her involved, it might escalate into something that prevented me from transferring.

"Alright, honey, let me think about it. Go to school today if you're up to it. We'll talk later tonight."

The last place I wanted to be was in school, so I took my mom's initial advice and took the day off. I wasn't skipping school without a purpose, however; I knew exactly where I was headed. Part two of my plan.

When I arrived at Luther's workshop, he greeted me at the door wearing a navy blue military style blazer. It was fitted to accentuate the narrowness of his waist, and the flare at the bottom was enough to suggest that it was definitely not made for men.

"Chloe-Grace, delighted to see you! It's been way too long."

"Luther, I just saw you last week."

"Like I said, entirely too long," he said, smiling. "Come on in!"

Luther's workshop used to be a small garment factory. He had gutted the place and put in a series of windows along the top of the walls to let in natural light. Two antique wooden fans spun lazily over worktables strewn with patches of cloth, as haughty-looking mannequins stood around in various states of undress.

I followed Luther in and immediately started going through the racks of clothes he always had on display. I stopped and picked out an oversized Asian-print blouse. "This is amazing. Where'd you get this?"

"Oh, I don't know. I just picked it up somewhere. Try it on. If you like, you can have it."

I smiled. I loved coming to Luther's.

I put the blouse back on the rack and turned to him. "Actually, Luther, I'm here because I need your help."

"Doesn't everybody!" he said, rolling his eyes in mock exasperation.

"Seriously. I need you to be my fairy godmother. But in reverse."

"What do you mean?" he asked, looking at me quizzically.

"I need to become a pumpkin." I had planned to use this exact phrase because I knew that anything Cinderella-related would strike a chord with Luther.

"Become a pumpkin? My God! Why in the world would you want to become a pumpkin? Fairy godmothers are there to protect you and make you look amazing. I've never heard of one that turns somebody into a pumpkin. That sounds more like a witch." Luther pulled up two high-back chairs, and we both sat down.

I continued, "Well, the short story is that I'm transferring schools next week and I need to be totally unrecognizable. I can't be Chloe-Grace anymore. I want a whole new me." Okay, I realized my mom still hadn't officially said yes. But in the past her "thinking about it" was essentially the same as "yes." Coming to Luther was just to get a head start on the process.

Luther looked confused and concerned. "Is this some sort of prequarter-life crisis I'm not aware of? Why are you transferring schools?" He narrowed his eyes. "Okay, enough beating around the bush. Spill it. What's going on?"

I took a deep breath and let it out. "I'm just sick of it. I'm sick of being Chloe-Grace. I'm sick of the cameras, the false stories, the fake people. I'm tired of it all. I just want to be anonymous, to be a nobody. So I decided I should transfer schools, see what it's like to be normal. Just try it out for a while." I purposefully left out the part about my brother. I love Luther, and he is discreet; but he is also close with my mom. There would be no way he could (or would) keep such a secret.

"And your parents—what do they think?"

"My mom's still thinking about it, which means yes. My dad— well, he doesn't know."

Luther looked at me incredulously.

"Anyway, it doesn't matter. I've made up my mind."

Luther was quiet for a minute, then looked at me and smiled. "Okay, and my role in this?"

"I need to look totally unrecognizable. Can you do it?"

Springing up from his chair, Luther started to pace in front of me. "Can I do it? Chloe-Grace, do you know who you're talking to? Of course I can do it! I transformed your mother into that hideous-looking creature for her Oscar win. Remember? If I can do that, I can certainly make you into Susie Nobody. I'm just not sure that I should. I mean, you mom hasn't said yes. Your dad doesn't have a clue. . . ."

"Please, Luther? My mom will say yes. You know that. And forget my dad. Besides, it'll be like a challenge." I got out of my chair to grab his hand to make him stop pacing. "Think of how much fun it'll be. I'll let you do whatever you want."

"Anything I want?"

I smiled, knowing I had just won over Luther.

"Anything you want," I said sweetly.

He paused and sighed in mock resignation. "Fine. You've got yourself a deal, young lady. Now, explain what you mean by 'pumpkin.'" Luther stopped pacing and perched himself on a wrought iron spiral staircase that sat in the middle of the room overlooking the work floor, its steps leading up to his outfitting room.

"Basically, I want to blend in with everyone. You know, look normal." I went to stand next to him.

"Ugh, why would you want to be normal? I grew up normal, and let me tell you, the experience is way overrated." I couldn't imagine Luther growing up normal. In my conception of Luther, I envisioned him just springing out into the world as this fantastic stylist creature.

"Isn't it true that you always want what you don't have?" I said firmly.

"Chloe dear, you have everything. What could you possibly want?"

"Anonymity."

That made him laugh.

"Okay. Fine, you want to look like a local. Where are you transferring to?"

"Hollis."

"Is that where your mom is staying for her next movie? It sounds so quaint. Where is that? Somewhere in England? Scotland? Oooh, Italy?" He clapped his hands in delight.

"Not quite. It's in Alhambra." I shrugged apologetically.

Luther scrunched up his nose. "Why in the world are you transferring to a slum?"

For the record, Alhambra is not an actual physical slum. Luther meant *slum* in the fashion sense, about which he was probably one hundred percent correct.

"I decided I just want to get away to the most unassuming place I could think of," I said, as we moved up the stairs. The outfitting room is filled with mirrors and arching lights, making it look like an entire dressing room had been ripped out and transported upstairs.

"So, you're hiding out, huh?"

"Not really. I prefer to think of it as a fresh start. I'm not hiding from anyone, except maybe the paparazzi. But it would be like a new beginning."

"And who's going to know about this? Just wee little me?"

"I'm hoping as few people as possible. So please keep it a secret, okay?" I plopped myself down on the couch and sunk in among the throw pillows.

"How about I'll keep it a secret if you tell me what's really going on."

I glanced down at my hands. I had been absentmindedly pulling on the loose seam of one of the pillows.

"I told you. I'm sick of everything, Luther. I just want to get away from all this stuff that's been happening. From dealing with Mom and Dad, and all the stupid people at Newton. I want to know what it's like *not* to be Chloe-Grace. To see what it would be like to be perfectly normal. Maybe even a nobody."

"I still don't know why anyone would aspire to be 'normal,' but fine. Let's see what I can do."

We looked over the racks of clothes he had upstairs. "Don't you have anything that's not so trendy and fabulous?"

"Who do you think you're talking to? Everything I touch becomes trendy."

"Okay, fine. Do you have anything you haven't Midas touched around here?"

Pausing to think for a moment, Luther replied, "I do have boxes of junk that people send me. They hope I'll use them in movies or something. I don't even look at them twice because they're so hideous." He went to the corner of the room and lifted out two boxes that were stacked in the back.

I looked in one of them and saw an unorganized pile of clothes that had names I'd normally faint at. Steeling myself, I pulled out a pair of no-name jeans. The color was all wrong and the cut way so two seasons ago, but I tried them on.

After changing, I stepped in front of the mirrors. I turned a little so I could get the back view. Way too baggy in the butt, and they were too short even though I was wearing my sequined ballet flats.

"How do I look?" I grinned, knowing full well what he would say.

"Honestly?"

"This isn't completely ugly."

"Well, it's hardly flattering." He sighed and scrunched up his face in disgust. "I think we can still get away with some style. Just take it a bit more casual. Try this on." He handed me a slightly rumpled pair of True Religion jeans off the rack and yanked a scoop neck tee out of the box. "There's no need to have no style whatsoever."

I was relieved to put on something that fit correctly.

I spent the rest of the afternoon trying on things that weren't obviously designer or overly trendy: a cool pair of Converse sneakers, some J.Crew pants, and a stack of Gap tees with semicool designs stamped on them.

Finally, Luther looked at me and said, "Well, it's not designer, but it'll do. Friends don't let friends be ugly, even if they ask for it. Now, about that hair. We're going to need to cut it if you really want to change your look. What do you think?"

Knowing that this would be coming, I brushed my hands through my long hair one last time and said without hesitation, "Yes, please."

A few hours later, with my hair all chopped off and cropped, I could feel the air around my bare neck. Luther decided that a drastic new haircut would be the key to my transformation. My slightly wavy, long hair had been straightened and trimmed into a sloping haircut with bangs in the front and a slight bob in the back. I felt like a completely different person already. I couldn't wait to get home and show my mom.

She was stretched out on a patio chair, and as I walked outside, she looked up from the book she was reading. She squinted as she took in my new hairstyle. "I guess if you're looking for big change, that's a good place to start," she said.

"So you've decided that I can transfer?" I knew I sounded overly hopeful, as if my happy enthusiasm would make the decision for her.

"Well, you've already cut your hair. What if I said no? You'd grow it back?"

Still getting used to how short it was, I couldn't keep from swishing it back and forth, reveling in how free I felt. "I kind of like it this way."

She looked at me appraisingly. "Luther did a nice job."

"He called you?"

"Of course he did. He told me all about your . . . What did he call it? A makeunder? Very cute."

"Did he tell you why?"

"You want to become a normal girl. A Plain Jane who can blend in with any girl on the street." She marked the place in her book and set it down, sitting up in the process. I was glad at this moment I hadn't told Luther about my other family.

"And you understand now?" I hoped that talking to Luther had given her another perspective. She was so used to hearing his voice about what she needed to be doing with her hair, makeup, and outfits that he was able to subtly influence her in some other areas too. He used this power sparingly, of course, and only in the service of her glamorousness. Or in this case, for me.

My mom sighed. "Yes, I get it. The news about the divorce has been difficult, your father could hardly be worse, you're feeling like everything around you is falling apart. You're stressed out and worried." Taking a moment to look carefully at me, she added, "I'm just concerned that this is a bit too much. Transferring to another school anonymously? That sounds drastic."

"Mom, seriously, it's not. I've been thinking about it, and I really think this will be the best thing for me. I've never been away from the people at Newton, and I'm getting sick of them."

Knowing that I would have to do some final convincing, I pulled out all my acting abilities, pretending this was one of those legal movies and I was a lawyer about to make her case in front of the jury. "Haven't you ever felt like you just needed to get away? Remember telling me about how you just hated growing up in your small town? You didn't even finish high school before you left."

My mom was surprised to hear me bring up her childhood. "I left to became an actress, Chloe. It's not exactly the same thing when I had a goal and a dream. You can't be an actress in the middle of nowhere Michigan. I had to leave."

"No, you CHOSE to leave. Which is what I'm doing. I'm choosing to transfer schools." I was pleading now, knowing that by drawing parallels to her escape from the Midwest I'd strike a deep chord with my mom. "I just want to give it a try. See if it'll be better."

Eyes lifted toward the sky, my mom didn't say anything for a few minutes. Finally, she took a deep breath. "Fine. If that's what you really want, you can transfer."

"Yes!" I ran over and gave her a huge hug of gratitude.

She swept the hair out of my eyes. "You know, I had been thinking of taking you to Capri with me on your spring break. I start shooting next week for a new movie. But now I have a better idea. We'll say that you're coming with me for the whole semester. That'll take you out of school for a while so you can go on your little adventure. Plus, it will get the paparazzi to focus on Europe, not here. If you really want to be anonymous, you have to do it right. How's that sound?"

This was getting better by the second. My mom had taken me seriously and actually listened to me. I looked at her apprecia- tively. "If you're going to Capri, where will I stay?"

"Luther said he'd take you in. He's not coming with me. If he's going to wardrobe you, you might as well live with him."

I couldn't stop a huge grin from appearing on my face. "Luther is going to take me in? Is he sure he wants to do that?"

My mom's face matched mine. "He says it'll be exciting to have someone to tuck in at night. He said it'll be like harboring a fugitive. He can keep an eye on you too."

"Totally, I can deal with that."

So that was it. I had my new clothes, my new hair, my mom's permission, and a new life to look forward to. I should have done this years ago. After working out some details about what we'd need to do in order to prepare for the transition, I went upstairs to tell Vickie the exciting news.

"Wait, so are you still going to go by Chloe?" she asked after I was done filling her in on the finer details of my plan. She couldn't believe I was going to transfer to another school. I felt a little bad ditching her, but I knew she'd understand.

"Actually, I thought about that. I think I'm going to have to change it. It's too conspicuous. I was thinking of going by Lilly."

"Cool, good name. Lilly it is. Do you want me to start calling you that to get you used to it?" Vickie was way on top of this.

"Great idea. I'd better start having everyone call me Lilly."

Well, not everybody, just Luther and Vickie. Aside from my mom, I had decided that nobody needed to know what I was doing, especially not Rachelle. I felt bad about not telling Rachelle everything, but I knew that there was no way she could keep a secret like this.

"Oh, and I'm not telling Rachelle, by the way," I confessed.

"Really?" Vickie sounded really surprised. "But she's your best friend; won't she feel offended?"

"Well, I'm not sure I can trust her not to let anything slip. I mean, I know you'd never say anything to anyone; but with Rachelle, she just lacks discretion sometimes. I kind of feel like she'd be more interested in throwing a going-away party or something. I'm just going to pretend I'm really in Capri and still e-mail her and stuff."

"Wow, okay. So I'm the only person at school who'll know?"

"Vick, you'll be like one of the only people who'll know, period. So, thank you so much for everything. You've been an amazing friend through all this. I'm not sure I would have been able to do this without you."

I could almost hear Vickie's smile over the phone. "Lilly, it's been my pleasure. Call me if you need anything, okay?"

And with that I got ready to let my Chloe life go and my Lilly life begin.

# Chapter
## *8*

"Lilly! We're going to be late if you don't hurry up," Luther yelled from downstairs.

It was Monday morning, the first day of my new life, and I was already late. After mom approved my transfer, I'd spent the next week moving into Luther's and amassing a wardrobe of "normal" clothes. I'd also spent an entire day convincing Rachelle I was off to Capri. Needless to say, she was überjealous.

And now here I was, ready with my freshly sharpened generic pencils and boring notebooks, excited to start my new life. I finished getting dressed and put on my makeup. My new makeup scheme called for much less than I normally used. You would think less makeup would make the application process faster, but I kept changing my mind. Obviously running out of time, I decided just to go with some mascara and lip gloss and hoped that would be different enough from the usual Chloe look.

"Gimme a sec, I'll be right there," I yelled back.

Living with Luther had been quite the experience. He really seemed to revel in his new role as fake parent and had gone out of his way to simulate a normal home environment. I kept telling him that I've had anything but a normal home life, but he said that since I was going to be a normal girl now, I needed a normal lifestyle too.

He even set up daily dinnertimes, a curfew, a homework hour, and a no-TV-until-everything-is-done rule. A color-coded chores schedule was tacked onto the door of the fridge. I wasn't sure if Luther really meant for me to follow any of the "rules," but the effort he made was amusing, and touching.

As I finally arrived downstairs in my official first-day-of-new-school outfit—black skinny jeans, a pink hoodie, and a vintage Jem & the Holograms T-shirt—I was startled to see Luther in a double-breasted suit and horrific striped tie.

When he saw me come in, he did a slow twirl. "How do I look?"

"Terrible." I couldn't help laughing. "Why in the world are you dressed like that?"

"I can't very well take you to school dressed like my normal fabulous self. If you're going Vanilla Jane, I'm dressing down too." Luther was going to drive me to school today to finish up some paperwork. He looked hilariously unfashionable and certainly ready to play the part of Daddy Dearest.

"Wait, did you dye your hair?" Luther's dark black hair was tinged with a hint of gray at the temples.

He gingerly touched the sides of his head. "Oh, that. It's just spray on. I would look way too young to have a daughter your age otherwise."

"Oh, I think you'll blend right in." I just hoped I would. My biggest worry was that my disguise would be inadequate and people would see right through the new hair, makeup, and clothes. I made sure to grab my biggest pair of sunglasses as we headed out the door. Maybe I should have picked a hat to hide under. Too late now.

As we drove within sight of Hollis High, my stomach started getting uncomfortably tight, and I had to roll down the window an inch for some air. Facing a red carpet with thousands of people screaming my name didn't make me this nervous. I tried to settle down as we queued up to get into the student parking lot. A line of ten cars stretched ahead of us just to get to the gate. This never happened at Newton. In fact, Hollis High's parking lot seemed incredibly huge for a high school. We ended up parking so far away from the entrance, I felt as if we had just arrived at Disneyland.

Luther must have thought the same thing, because he took out his cell phone and snapped a picture of where we parked. He turned to me and joked, "Should we wait for the tram?"

I smiled. But hesitating, I stopped to look around at all the kids. This was more overwhelming than I had anticipated.

"Lilly, stop that. You look like a big tourist. Come on." He took my hand and started marching us toward the entrance.

"Luther, I don't think high schoolers walk into school holding their daddy's hand."

"How cute. I'm embarrassing you already." He dropped

my hand and fell two steps behind me. "Lead the way, young lady."

As we walked, I swear people looked my way and pointed me out to their friends. I was too afraid to return their looks, even for a second, and hoped it was just new-girl attention. We made it to the entrance without any cries of recognition, so I let my paranoia simmer down a little.

A uniformed security guard—an actual security guard; this definitely wasn't Newton—opened the door for us as we approached. He nodded politely to Luther as he waved us inside.

As we walked down the hall toward the administration office, Luther leaned toward me and whispered, "I can't believe you want to come here. It's so grimy, and everything looks disheveled."

In comparison to Newton, Hollis *was* bare-bones and devoid of much decoration. The hallways were covered with utilitarian tiles, and the lockers were a hideous ocher color. Butcher paper-and student-created signs were the only things hanging on the walls. This was a far cry from Newton's award-winning interiors.

So this was how the other half lived. No wood trim on the ceilings, not one design flourish to be found. The whole place looked . . . institutional. Newton already felt like a whole world away. I smiled. "It's perfect."

As soon as we entered the administration office, Luther made it a point to say loud and clear, "Lillian Chen is here. We're new, and she needs to get all set up."

Of course, the only person inside was a bored-looking receptionist, so Luther sounded incredibly silly announcing our presence to a near empty room. I tugged his arm. "Luther! Don't go overboard, please."

I faced the receptionist and smiled. "Hi, I'm Lilly."

"I know." She rolled her eyes. "I heard him the first time." Plucking a well-worn clipboard off a nearby shelf, she handed it to us along with some forms. "Go ahead and have a seat. Fill these out. Mrs. Guerra, our student counselor, will be right with you."

As we sat down, Luther reached into the hidden jacket pocket of his suit and pulled out a thin pen, pink and glittery, with a small tassled pom-pom at the top. Without a pause he started to fill out the forms. I looked up at the receptionist, sure that she would have noticed. Luckily, she wasn't paying any further attention to us, so I jumped up to snatch a plain black pen from her desk.

"Let's use this one, okay?" I said, handing him the pen.

Looking at the pink pen in his hand as if it had magically appeared, Luther mouthed, "Sorry."

As soon as he finished the paperwork, I nudged Luther and said, "You can go now."

"What? You don't want me to stick around?"

"No, I think I can take it from here. Thanks."

"Okay, fine. Have a good day, sweetie. I'll pick you up at three."

I gave him a hug as he left. I reviewed what Luther had written on the forms until Mrs. Guerra was ready for me.

As soon as I got into her cramped, boring office (which was the antithesis of Ms. Wenter's over-the-top office), Mrs. Guerra exuded a sense of motherly calm. After some quick introductions, she asked me why I was transferring so late into the school year. "It's highly unusual, you know."

Stumbling over my words while thinking of an adequate answer, I said, "My dad got a new job and we just moved. And, um, it was too far to take the bus to school from across town." I hoped she wouldn't ask where we had moved from or which buses I had in mind because, of course, I knew nothing about buses anywhere.

I realized I was going to have to think fast on my feet the first few days here and get my backstory straight. I had been so focused on disguising my looks, I had forgotten to think about what I would say to people when they asked about why I was here.

"Well, I'm sure you'll do just fine, Lilly." She closed my file on her desk. "Let me find someone to show you around."

She pushed a button on her phone, and the intercom speaker crackled to life. Her voice piped over it loud and clear. "Can I get Jana C. to report to the office, please. Jana C."

Mrs. Guerra turned her attention back to me. "Jana's also a junior, and she's one of our academic buddies. We don't have a schedule for you yet, but you can just follow Jana around today, if that's alright."

"Of course, no problem."

The orientation information I received from Mrs. Guerra consisted of a map of the school and that was about it. The prospect of having someone to show me around the first day made me a little less nervous.

A girl bounded into the office all breathless. Her straight black hair was streaked with blonde and she looked Asian, but not entirely. Maybe she was mixed? Her jeans had big holes casually ripped out from the knees, as if they were her favorite pair that she couldn't bear throwing away. She seemed to be really tan and toned, and she had on large white hoop earrings that matched the brightness of her wide smile. A smile that flashed only for a moment before it was replaced with deep concern.

"You needed me, Mrs. Guerra? Is something wrong?"

"Oh hi, Jana. I didn't mean for you to run here." As Mrs. Guerra stood up, I followed suit. "I want you to meet Lilly," she introduced me with a sweep of the arm. "She's just transferred here from Newton, and it's her first day. I wanted you to show her around."

All the tension in Jana's face melted, and she visibly relaxed. "Ohmigosh, I thought I was in trouble or something. I've never been called out of class like that before."

Still breathing hard, she extended her hand and gave me a broad smile. "Hi, Lilly, I'd be superhappy to show you around."

"Thanks!"

"I'm so sorry I was such a spaz back there," Jana said once we left Mrs. Guerra's office. "I just didn't know I was supposed to show someone around. I got all panicked when I heard my name over the loudspeaker. If they call you in the middle of class, that's usually bad."

"I'll make sure I never get called out of class," I said, and smiled. It was a lame comeback, but I had no idea what to say to her.

Even though she was right around my height, Jana took much longer strides than I did, and she scooted through the hallways quickly. I imagined she didn't want to miss any more class than she already had.

"So, Jana," I said, as I tried my best to keep pace. "How many kids are there at Hollis?" I wanted to know how big a pond I had just jumped into.

Slowing down a half step, she thought about it for a moment. "I think two thousand or so. I'm not sure. The classes keep getting bigger each year. I know there's around four hundred juniors."

"Wow." The entire high school population of Newton was just over five hundred students. I thought about how I would find my brother in this sea of students. Maybe Jana knew him? Although the chances of a junior knowing some random freshman seemed pretty slim. It might seem weird for me to ask about it now, anyway. I decided to see what I could do on my own. Or maybe wait until I knew Jana better.

We arrived at the door to a classroom, and Jana twisted the handle but paused before opening it. "Ready?"

I nodded as she pushed open the door and ushered me in. The first thing I noticed was that the classroom was packed; and as soon as we entered, everyone swiveled in his or her seat to stare. Great. Thirty people looking at me at once. It would just take one pair of eyes to notice and point out that maybe I looked a lot like Chloe-Grace to ruin everything.

Cutting my hair short seemed like a terrible idea now. I should have kept it long to hide my face a little.

"Mr. Carter, everybody, this is Lilly. She just transferred in today," Jana said as a murmur washed over the crowd. I gave what I hoped was a friendly wave to everyone.

"Welcome, Lilly," Mr. Carter said enthusiastically. "Feel free to take a seat anywhere. The period's almost over." He resumed talking about the Pythagorean theorem as Jana and I settled into two desks near the back. Before I could properly get my bearings, the bell rang. The whole room practically jumped up at once, nobody even giving me a second glance in the rush to leave.

"I've got to grab my books." I followed Jana as she went to gather her books from her original seat up in the first row.

"So, Lilly, how was math class at your last school? Were you in geometry?" Mr. Carter waddled over near us.

"Yeah, I was." Actually, we had already covered what he had just been talking about three weeks ago at Newton.

"I'm sure you'll do just fine here. Jana will show you everything you need to know." He gave her a bright smile. "She's a star here."

Blushing, Jana said, "Please, that's so not true." She headed toward the door. "Okay, let's go. See you later, Mr. C."

I dutifully followed her out.

I shadowed Jana all morning, and she remained unfailingly nice throughout. She always took a seat as smack-dab up front and to the middle as possible and started by introducing me around before each class. Three morning classes meant three chances to be presented in front of an engaged audience, and I was sure I was the object of some scrutiny each time, especially since we sat in such conspicuous places. Still, by the time ninety people had had their chance to study me with no repercussions, I felt pretty confident in my Lilly getup.

Well, that was, until lunch. It all started when Jana's friends, all of them disarmingly nice, had asked where I transferred from. Stupidly, I blurted out Newton. I didn't think I could get away with saying anything else, because I didn't have a clue what other schools were like and I couldn't very well pretend to be from a place I knew nothing about.

"That's where all the celebrity kids go, right." Brett, sitting two seats down on my left, jumped into the conversation. His question was totally rhetorical. The only person at the table who didn't know Newton was "Celebrity High" happened to be Jana, who didn't seem to be much into that kind of stuff.

"You transferred from Newton to here? Why?" I gave them the same wimpy answer I had given Mrs. Guerra a few hours earlier about my father moving and it being too far of a commute.

One of the girls, Angela, looked as if she was now hanging on my every word. "So, what was it like? Who do you know there? Anyone famous?"

I squirmed.

I had pegged myself as not just "Lilly the new girl" but "Lilly the new girl who had transferred from Newton, high school of the rich and famous." I was stuck. I didn't want to admit that I knew anybody there at all. It might be incriminating.

"Well . . . " I paused to buy some time. "I just didn't really fit in. I think people didn't like me. . . ." My voice trailed off as I glanced uncomfortably down at my hands, realizing I sounded totally lame.

"I knew it!" Stefanie, who was sitting across from me, exclaimed. I looked up with fear. "I heard all those Newton kids were supersnobby. My friend's cousin goes there, and she said that nobody gives you the time of day unless your parents are somebody."

She looked at me for confirmation. "I'll bet you hated it there because they just thumbed their snooty noses at you, right? Everyone's totally bitchy, I'm sure."

My eyes widened in surprise, and my mouth dropped open. *Was this what all other kids thought about Newton? Everyone there was automatically bitchy?* Actually, thinking of Stacey Macedo, and even Rachelle on some of her finer days, that assumption might not have been too far off.

By my reaction, Stefanie realized that what she said could have been taken the wrong way. She quickly added, "Oh no. I don't mean everyone. You seem really nice, Lilly." She blushed apologetically.

I gave her a forgiving smile and then, not wanting to ignore the life preserver she'd thrown me, said, "Yeah, some of the people there are, like, totally bitchy."

Angela added, "And spoiled too, I'd bet. I saw this one episode of *Super Sweet Sixteen* where this girl got a Range Rover for her birthday, but she cried because it wasn't her favorite color."

That was Susan McAdams's birthday party last year, and I'd actually thought it was kind of wrong that her parents had gotten her a white car and not blue like she'd wanted. Not that I was going to admit to that now.

"I would've loved to have gotten something like that for my birthday," Angela continued. "I barely got a cake and use of my parents' car on the weekends."

The rest of lunch breezed by as I safely dodged more questions about who I knew at Newton by telling them about how most kids there were more concerned with their BMWs than ABCs. I told them about the free cupcakes and the valet parking, and some of the pretentious things that I actually quite liked about Newton, but spun out in a new, disapproving light. Hey, when in Rome, right?

By the end of the school day, I started to feel as if I had found a great group of people to hang out with. I was quite proud actually.

Luther was still in his suit and tie when he picked me up. Jana and Stefanie had been nice enough to wait with me, and I waved good-bye to them as I slid into the passenger seat.

"Look at that. My little girl already made new friends." He gave Jana and Stefanie the once-over before we drove off. "Is that girl really wearing gladiator sandals? Blech. So over."

"Be nice. They're totally great, and just because they don't maintain your fashion standards doesn't make them bad people."

Luther turned to give me a look of mock astonishment. "Well, well. Look at you, Ms. Fashion Proletariat. Don't you mean *our* fashion standards?"

"Well, yeah. But you know, not everyone here is the same, okay?"

"I guess you won't be needing this then?" Reaching an arm into the backseat, he grabbed something and tossed it in my lap.

"A Marc Jacobs backpack? Lilly can't use this."

He shushed me. "Please. Tell everyone it's a fake. Nobody here would be able to tell the difference anyway."

I couldn't help laughing. "You've got a good point there." I had to agree with Luther that Hollis was definitely missing the fashion sophistication of Newton, but that was part of what made it feel so thrillingly different.

After just one day it already felt as if I was in a whole new world, as if this was a place where I could be anyone I wanted to be. Hundreds of kids, and nobody would know who I was unless I wanted them to. What a novelty!

# Chapter
## 9

Still giddy from the newness of it all, I spent most of the morning of my second day following Jana around again. But before I got completely comfortable being Jana's sidekick, Mr. Levitz, Hollis's other guidance counselor, called me in to talk about what classes would make up my new schedule.

After I spent most of the afternoon taking assessment tests, it turned out I was quite the excellent student (of course). I tested into four advanced classes. That was the good part. Then Mr. Levitz asked what sorts of extracurriculars I was involved in at my old school. Naively I had said chorus, and before I caught myself, my sixth-period class was Music, and I was stuck back in another musical despite my horrendous singing voice.

"You're in a musical again?" Vickie asked when I called her after school. "I thought you went to this school to get away from everything you did before. You don't even like singing!"

"Tell me about it."

"Well, I guess some things don't change, huh?" she continued, chuckling.

"Vickie, you aren't helping." The idea of having to sing and embarrass myself at another school was cringe inducing.

I could hear Vickie trying to muffle her laughter. "Well, aside from that, how's everything else going?"

"Well, they seem to think we're all snobby over at Newton, that's for sure." I quickly filled in Vickie on what happened during my first two days at Hollis, especially about how the girls had said that Newton students were so snooty and obnoxious.

"It's hard to blame them, I guess. Newton is pretty snobby," Vickie admitted. "I mean, everyone here is all about who has what and who knows who."

"Except for you," I pointed out.

"And you. You weren't really like that either." As she said this, I thought about it. There were certainly a lot of people I'd never paid much attention to, and at one point in time that had probably included Vickie.

"I kind of was. I think that by having Rachelle as a friend, I'd always just automatically filtered who we shouldn't hang out with." I had always assumed it was because we didn't have anything in common with the people we excluded. I saw now that that probably wasn't it. Having common interests didn't make you best friends or, more importantly, close friends.

"No, you've always been nice, at least," Vickie replied. "You just weren't always that approachable maybe." She was right.

I regretted not giving more people a chance back at Newton. What if that kind of attitude had prevented me from getting to know Vickie, who was such a great person even if we were totally different?

"Anyway, on to Newton gossip. You know Austin and Stacey broke up, right?"

Somehow the news didn't affect me in any way. I replied sarcastically, "Were they really even together?"

"Ha, totally. Sorry, I won't bother giving you Austin updates. I just thought maybe you'd want to know."

"Thanks for thinking about it that way. To be honest, I don't want to think about him at all. I just want to concentrate on my new school."

"Speaking of that, did you find your brother yet?"

I shifted my phone to my other ear. "It's only been two days. I'm a little worried, though, because the school's, like, really big. There's two thousand people there, and I only have a few pictures of him to go by."

"Maybe you can look him up in the yearbook?" she suggested helpfully.

"I tried that already. Didn't work. He's a freshman, so he wasn't in last year's yearbook."

"Do any of your new friends know him?"

"I don't know. I've been afraid to ask. I mean, I just met them. It'd be kind of weird if I asked if they knew some random freshman, right?"

"That's true. Well, give it a few more days. I'm sure you'll run into him at some point."

"True," I replied.

Luther walked in waving his arms and pointing to his watch, which meant "homework time." He really was taking this "dad" thing too seriously.

I nodded and waved him off. "Listen, I gotta go," I said to Vickie. "Luther is playing disciplinarian dad, and I need to do some homework. I'll talk to you later."

"Okay. But keep me updated, especially about your brother."

"I will," I replied, and clicked off my phone.

My disappointment in not being able to find my brother didn't last long. The next day, in my new Honors Geometry class, Mr. Ramirez asked me to come up to the front of the class for introductions.

"Hi, my name is Lillian Chen. I just transferred here and—" As I was forced to introduce myself yet again, I saw him. My brother, sitting right in my class. I was surprised and froze up. "Um, yeah, and um, that's it."

"Okay, great, thanks, Lillian," Mr. Ramirez said. "Everyone, please make her feel welcome."

As I walked back to my desk, I tried not to stare at him. I passed his desk and carefully looked over just to see if I could confirm my suspicions, and there it was: HONG-YIN, written in clear block letters on his paper. *Ohmigod! I found him!* As I took my seat two desks behind him, I tried to get a better look at him. He was awfully skinny and a bit dorky, and looked as if he still belonged in middle school. His teal-and-white striped sweater seemed to be way too big and was hopelessly out of date. But despite this lack of fashion sense, I couldn't believe my luck! Having a class with him would make getting to know him so much easier.

The next thing I knew, the girl sitting in front of me turned around. "Hey, Lilly, right? I'm Hannah."

"Uh, hi. Nice to meet you," I said, turning my full attention toward her. "So, what are we doing now?" I'd been too busy getting over my shock at seeing Hong-Yin to actually pay attention to what Mr. Ramirez had said.

"We're pairing up for the class assignment. Don't worry about it, though. It's supereasy," she said breezily. "The answers for the even-numbered problems are in the back." She flipped the textbook open and showed me.

"Cool." Normally I would have objected to taking the easy way out, but I had more important things on my mind. "Do you guys do this a lot? I mean, get together during class to do projects and stuff."

"Yeah, like every day. Mr. Ramirez is a superlaid-back teacher. If he doesn't give us an assignment, we can just work on our homework." Hannah's glasses slipped down her nose, and she absentmindedly pushed them back up.

Perfect. My plan for getting to know Hong-Yin became clear. I would just have to make sure that we were paired up for assignments. Then we could become friends and then siblings and then . . . I smiled brightly at Hannah. "So you can just pick whoever you want to work with?"

"Well, it's usually whoever you're sitting next to. That's my friend Christina over there." I looked over to where she had quickly pointed. A large, scary-looking girl with fierce bangs was sitting across from Hong-Yin. "We usually try to sit next to each other, but I came in late today."

"Who's that she's partnered up with? He looks like he's scared of her." Hong-Yin was sitting as far away from Christina as possible, looking as if he needed an eject button on his chair.

"Oh, that's just Hong-Yin. But everyone calls him Henry. He's like supersmart but totally weird. He doesn't talk or something. Last time I worked with him he kept saying 'Okay, okay, okay.' It got kind of annoying after a while." She looked up with a mischievous smile. "Why, do you think he's cute or something?"

Ah, no. "I was just wondering because, you know, he looks sort of out of place here."

"Oh, he's not supposed to be here. He's a freshman. He's just in our class because he's, like, smart."

"Gotcha. Good to know."

For the rest of class, Hannah and I worked on our assignment, and right as we finished, the bell rang. Henry snatched up his backpack and ran out the door.

"Thanks for your help, Hannah. See you later," I said, quickly grabbing my things and heading out after Hong-Yin, I mean "Henry." Gotta remember that.

He was already halfway down the hall, deftly navigating his way through the crowd. Getting a better look at him, I shook my head at his choice of jeans. The wash was all wrong, the fit was too tight, and, worst of all, they were tapered at the bottom. *Tapered!*

I followed Henry all the way to his locker and watched as he grabbed a lunch bag and then raced away. A sense of relief came over me from finding him so soon. It felt like perfect karma that we were in the same class, giving me a chance to get to know him without making some sort of manufactured effort. Well, not totally manufactured, anyway. Tomorrow I'd still have to get to class and make sure to sit next to him. But this would be so much easier.

I turned and made my way down the hall toward my next class. I pulled out my cell phone and quickly texted Vickie. I had to share my excitement.

I found him! He's in my geometry class! Details later.

Her reply was just a string of excited exclamation marks and a big smiley face—exactly how I felt.

My morning classes ended, and I headed to the cafeteria for lunch. After my first two days at Hollis, I'd been happily adopted into Jana's group of friends and went to find their table in the cafeteria.

I was still getting used to the differences between Newton and Hollis. Back at Newton we didn't have a cafeteria, just a row of food vendors like you'd find at a mall food court. The few tables in the immediate area were never used because everyone just bought his or her food and then scattered to sit elsewhere on campus.

Hollis was way different. Here I was, standing in front of the cafeteria, and I suddenly realized exactly what it felt like not to have a best friend around.

Just as I was about to turn around and leave, Stefanie saw me and waved me over. I didn't know it would be such a relief to see some familiar faces.

Walking over to the table, I was surprised to see that Stefanie was dressed in a cheerleader outfit. She didn't strike me as the type. Angela was sitting next to her, engrossed in a magazine.

"Hey, I didn't know you were a cheerleader," I said to Stefanie as I sat down. "How come you're over here and not sitting with the rest of your squad?" I noticed that there was a table of cheerleaders at the far end of the cafeteria.

"Oh, that's for the girls on varsity. I'm just on JV. We're not allowed to sit with them."

"Seriously?" I looked over at the girls across the room. Nothing remarkable seemed to stand out about them.

"There's a very strict cheerleader hierarchy," Angela explained, her frizzy blonde head rising up from her magazine to join in the conversation. "You don't make it to varsity unless they select you. Junior varsity is like the proving ground to see if you're cool enough."

"Cool enough to what?"

"To be a cheerleader."

"And that's like the most popular thing here?"

"Of course." They both looked at me as if it was the most self-evident thing in the world. "Wasn't it at Newton?"

"Not at all. Anyone could be a cheerleader. You just signed up." Usually our cheerleading team had to actively recruit participants. They tried to get me and Rachelle to join, but we had never even considered it. Who wanted to spend the afternoon practicing cheers for sports teams that never won? "It really wasn't that big of a deal."

"Well, the cheerleaders here are a big deal. At least the members of varsity are. JV not so much." Stefanie looked wistfully over at the far table. "I'm hoping they'll promote me next year."

Angela rolled her eyes, and I giggled as I unpacked my lunch. Yeah, I packed a lunch. Luther and I had gone to the store last night and picked out things for me to bring. At Newton, I'd always just bought things on campus, because the food was so good. After two days of eating Hollis's gut-wrenching cafeteria food, I knew I had to make a change. If I didn't bring my own food, I would likely starve.

"How come you don't do it, Angela?" I asked as I unwrapped my free-range turkey on whole-grain sandwich and lovingly inspected it before taking a bite.

"I wish. I can't dance a lick," she said. I smiled a little, thinking of Vickie. "I wish I could, though."

"Oh, I don't believe that. Everyone can dance. When we used to go out clubbing, that's all we'd do, no matter how bad we were."

They both looked at me, slightly surprised.

"You used to go clubbing?" Stefanie asked.

Whoops, major slipup. I had forgotten that normal high schoolers didn't get to go out to clubs. Racking my brain for an answer, I spit out, "Oh, I didn't mean real clubs. But sometimes there would be parties, you know. With, um, a clubbing theme." I cringed. That sounded so lame.

"Oh, so you went to awesome parties?" Angela asked, suddenly very interested.

"Well, I mean—"

"Hey, guys." *Oh thank goodness.* Jana walked over, giving me some time to think. Relieved to see her, I quickly asked, "Where've you been?"

"She's president of the do-gooder club," Stefanie said with mock sarcasm.

"It's called Key Club, thank you very much. We meet every Wednesday. Did you guys have something like that at Newton? You can join if you want. We do—"

Angela cut her off. "Lilly was telling us about how popular she was back at Newton."

Laughing and trying to play it off, I said, "I wasn't popular at all. All the cool kids had, like, famous parents and stuff. That was so not me." I hoped I was pulling this off convincingly. "People barely knew who I was."

"It's all pretty stupid. Angela and Stefanie are always talking about who's popular, who's cool, all that stuff," Jana said, rolling her eyes. "It's so boring."

"Oh, please. Jana just doesn't care because she didn't grow up here. She doesn't know what it's like to be a normal person." Angela said this teasingly, but Jana didn't seem to mind at all.

"I know how to be normal. I just don't care what everyone else thinks. Who cares who's popular? There're so many bigger things to be worried about. Like, you know, global warming. Hello?"

"Or how to make varsity," Stefanie said, giggling.

"You guys are hopeless."

I spent the rest of lunch listening to the girls continue to tease one another. As the lunch period ended, we were gathering our books when suddenly I was pushed into my table.

"What the—"

"Oh my gosh, I'm so sorry."

I looked up, and into the gorgeous green eyes of the cutest boy I'd seen at Hollis. He was tall and lanky, with a thin but pleasant face and a gorgeous head of dark, curly hair. I was rendered speechless.

"Hey, Jack, watch it," Jana answered, thankfully.

"I'm really sorry. It was Brett's fault," he said, giving a "you're dead" look to his friend.

I recovered as gracefully as I could and broke out my most winning smile. "It's fine. No worries."

Jack smiled at me for what seemed like forever until Angela cleared her throat and grabbed my arm.

"Come on, we'll be late to class. See ya, Jack."

I reluctantly followed. "Who was that?" I whispered.

"That's Jack—supercute, supereligible, but also superpicky. I don't think he's dated anyone other than a senior here—and he's only a sophomore," Stefanie explained.

"Yeah, don't even think about him. He's cute but unattainable," Angela added.

"Interesting," I replied. I smiled and walked with the girls to my next class. *Unattainable* was not in my vocabulary.

That night I recapped our whole lunch conversation to Vickie.

"This girl is really cool. Like, she cares about the environment, and she does all this community service stuff. I feel like she knows what she wants and doesn't let anything stop her."

"Well that's what you're doing, right? You know what you want, and you're not letting anyone stop you." This was true. I hadn't realized how cool it was that this was all actually happening.

"Oh, and I met this gorgeous boy—totally hot. He's deemed 'unattainable,' but we'll see."

"Wow, unattainable. That's quite a statement," Vickie said, "I'm guessing you'll be seeing if that's true?"

I smiled. "Maybe just a little."

"Good luck with that," Vickie said. "Guess what? They put me in one of the leads in the musical because Mandy Taylor broke her leg during field hockey. I feel kind of bad, but I'm kind of glad too, you know?"

Genuinely excited, I was delighted to share in some good news for Vickie. "That's so great! I knew there was no way they could keep you in the chorus. You're way too good for that."

"I wouldn't exactly call it starring, but at least it's better than the chorus. It'll be great."

"You're going to be simply amazing, I just know it." Taking a slight pause, I continued, "I have some more exciting news too—my brother."

"Ohmigosh, yes. Details, please."

"He was in my geometry class. I'm going to talk to him tomorrow."

"No way! What does he look like?"

"Well, he's a bit of a nerd, but he looks sweet."

"Are you nervous?"

"Not at all. I just hope he talks to me. Some girl in class was telling me how quiet he was." If there was one thing I knew how to do, though, it was talk to boys.

Following my thought exactly, Vickie said, "If anyone can get him to talk, you can. I can't wait for you to find out more about him."

"I know."

"Wow, you've been at your new school only a few days and it sounds like you love it. Things are really working out for you."

I couldn't help grinning to myself. If this was what normal was really like, I might never go back. "Okay, I gotta run. I'll call you in a few days. Wish me luck."

The next day in geometry class, I positioned myself right behind Henry, and we were paired together for the assignment. Hannah had raised her eyebrows at me when she saw Henry and me working together, but I pretended I didn't see her.

I scooted my desk next to Henry's. He looked even more uncomfortable than ever. I decided to go with the overfriendly "I'm new here" tactic to see if he'd talk. "Hey, I'm kind of new here, so maybe you can tell me how we should do this. Do you want to split up the problems, or maybe we can just do them all and then compare answers?"

He shifted in his chair and avoided making eye contact. "That sounds fine." He went right back to looking intently at his textbook.

"O-kay." Ugh, now what? I thought about trying to make small talk, but I looked at him and realized it was hopeless. I resigned myself to just working independently on the geometry problems. As I got to problem number two, I pushed too hard on my pencil and snapped it in half. Startled, Henry looked up.

"Shoot! Do you have another pencil?"

"You can use this one," he mumbled, offering me the pencil he was using.

"What are you going to use?"

He shrugged. "It's okay."

"No, I don't want to take your only pencil." I handed it back to him, but he didn't take it.

"I'm done already."

"What? You are?" I was surprised. "That was really fast. You're pretty good at this?"

"Well, my mom makes me go through everything earlier."

"What do you mean?" I asked.

He shifted his eyes downward and looked at his book. "I went through this chapter already. Like, last week." Then he added, "So you can use the pencil."

"Thanks." And that was it. I couldn't figure out what else to say to him the rest of class. He almost purposely refused to ask me any questions. I couldn't believe that I was here in the same class, sort of talking to my brother, and I couldn't get past the small talk. I realized I didn't exactly know how to talk to boys if I wasn't being just the tiniest bit flirty, something I couldn't do here, obviously. I decided that I was going to have to force the issue, since he might never talk to me if I didn't do something.

I went back to his blog Thursday night and scoured it for something to talk about with him. I decided that I would have to bring up a topic I was sure he had an opinion on.

During Friday's class, I made sure we were paired up again. Taking a deep breath, I opened my book and asked, "So, what are you doing this weekend? Are you going to watch that Blue Bomber movie?"

For the first time ever I saw my brother smile. He actually kind of made a noise like a giggle. "Blue Hornet, that's what you mean, right?"

"Right, that's the one."

"You don't know who he is?" He looked at me curiously.

I did since I'd read about him last night online, but I played dumb. "Nope, don't know a thing about it. What's the story?"

"The Blue Hornet's this guy who used to be just a nobody,

but he gets lost in the Egyptian desert and almost dies. But he's saved by an ancient race of people, and they give him all of these powers. Like he can fly and shoot things from his hands and . . ."

I smiled. My brother was talking. Finally. And even though I didn't care who the Blue whatever was, I was so happy I was finding out something about him. Having finally gotten him to talk, I wanted to keep it going. "That sounds really cool. Will it be good?"

"It's probably going to be the best movie ever. You should really go see it." He said this with serious conviction.

"Who're you going with?" I asked.

"My dad. He said he would take me, even if I wanted to watch it twice in a row." His dad, *our dad*, actually went with him to the movies? The only movies I'd ever gone out to with my parents were the ones my mom was in. Or sometimes their friends' premieres. But I didn't count those as spending time together because they were just there to promote or support, and they were constantly being interviewed before and afterward. We never went to see a movie just for the sake of it. I guess we couldn't really, because everyone would know who we were. Especially my mom.

"So, your dad is a fan too?"

Henry reached underneath his chair and got his backpack. "Not really, but I'm hoping he will be after he sees the movie. He only likes really old, boring movies and stuff. But I made him promise to watch this one with me."

Fishing around in his bag, he dug out a thin graphic novel. "Here, you can borrow this if you want." Turning shy again, he said, "If you think you'll like it, I mean."

I looked him straight in the eye and smiled. "Thanks. I'll definitely read it. And tell me how the movie is, okay? If it's really good, I'll check it out."

"Oh, it's going to be great. I promise."

It may not have been much, but I was delighted that we finally had a semireal conversation, even if it ended up being about something I had very little interest in. Flipping through the pages of the comic book as class ended, I knew it didn't matter. What was important was that we had finally talked, and that was a start.

For the last class of my first week at Hollis, I arrived at the music theater a few minutes early. I sat onstage, looking through the lyric book for Hollis's musical. Since I'd just transferred in, I was way behind in knowing the words. As I sang quietly out loud, out of nowhere someone said, "You're singing the wrong words."

I looked around, confused.

"Up here." A male voice drifted down toward me. I pulled my gaze way up into the rafters at the rear of the theater but couldn't make out anything in the darkness.

"I noticed that you've been singing the wrong words for rehearsal today. We'll be starting with the third song, not the second."

He was right, of course. I should've known that from the

announcement yesterday at the end of class. I'd been trying to stay as low-key as possible in my music class. I tried to whisper sing my way through each and every song I was in. I didn't think anyone would notice a background singer mumbling her way through a few lines. Apparently this guy was pretty observant.

I hoped he couldn't see me blushing from way up there.

"I'm sorry, I'm being rude. I'll be right down." His voice was already descending as I heard his footsteps thumping down the stairs. I really hoped he wasn't some weird maintenance guy. His voice sounded way too cute.

As he entered from the rear of the theater, my palms got a tad damp as I realized that the cute voice was attached to the cute guy from the cafeteria: Jack. He was dressed in loose jeans, black-and-white Chucks, and a brown hoodie.

He gave me a charmingly crooked smile.

"You aren't going to push me again, are you?"

"No, and I am sorry about that."

My heart started to flutter as I realized he was even cuter than I remembered from the cafeteria.

"Apology accepted," I flirted back. "Since when are you in this class? I haven't seen you here before."

"Actually, I'm in charge of running the spotlights for this show, so I technically don't come to class."

"Oh, so you just sit up there and spy on people, testing the lights every now and then," I said with a smirk.

"I only spy on some people, particularly those with vocal challenges."

"Hey, are you insulting my singing voice?" I asked incredulously.

"That's singing?" he said, laughing.

I smiled, trying to think of a witty retort. But just then some students entered the room, and Jack turned around to look at them.

"Alright, I gotta get back upstairs. Class is starting." He left with a sly wink and another flash of that crooked smile. Totally adorable.

Maybe the chorus wouldn't be so bad after all.

"Well, Ms. Lilly, aren't you just bursting with happiness. Good day?" Luther asked as I got into the car at the end of the day. I shut the door and waved to Jana, who was waiting for her ride.

"Let's just say that things are going really great. I met a cute boy in my last class, and Jana just invited me to join her tomorrow for a tree-planting day with her environmental club. It should be fun."

"Sounds like an eventful day. But tree planting? How 'Good Samaritan' of you."

"Yeah, not totally my idea of fun; but I'm Lilly now, not Chloe. Maybe Lilly will like being all 'green.'"

Luther smiled.

"Actually, I need to talk to you about something. I think I need a car. You've been driving me to school the entire week, and I know it's conflicting with your schedule. Plus, now that I have stuff to do on weekends, it would just be easier."

"That's fine, honey. You can take my car any time you want. There's a spare key in the glove compartment."

"That's a terrible place to keep a spare," I admonished. "Anyway, I can't drive your Beemer to school."

"Why not? I can rearrange my schedule. Is my car not good enough for you? Is it too embarrassing to drive Daddy Dearest's car?"

"Luther!" I exclaimed, laughing. "Of course it's not that. I just need to get around by myself. So, you know, I can do stuff after school. Hang out with people. Whatever."

Still pretending to be hurt, Luther gasped melodramatically. "I knew this day would come. I didn't think it would be so soon. I didn't even prepare for my empty nest. Soon I'll just be alone with my cats and my herbal tea and my empty, lonely rooms."

"You don't even have cats," I pointed out.

"I'd better get some then." Laughing, he said, "What kind of car did you want?"

"Anything that'll get me around, I guess. Something inconspicuous and regular. Nobody around here drives a BMW."

"When you said you needed a makeunder, you weren't kidding. Tell you what, I will find a wonderful, beat-up little thing. I'm sure there's a million of those around. We'll get you something by Monday."

Early Saturday afternoon, before Jana was scheduled to pick me up, I typed up a quick e-mail to Rachelle. This would be the first

Saturday brunch I'd missed with her and the girls in a while, and I didn't want her to think I didn't remember it.

Hey Rach, I hope you guys have an awesome time at brunch without me. Not too much though! Capri is great. Movie set is amazing. Say hi to Ashley and Joanna, okay? Love and kisses.

I shut my laptop just as Jana pulled up at the curb. I ran downstairs, shouted good-bye to Luther, and hopped in the car.

"Lilly! I'm so glad you could come today."

"Me too! Thanks for the invite."

"This will be a lot of fun. The group works around the city to plant trees alongside streets, campuses, and sometimes just in places that were burned by last year's fire. Today we're going to be planting fruit trees."

"Sounds great," I said, although I was still a little skeptical about the fun part.

We arrived ten minutes later and immediately got to work. Jana handed me a pair of thick work gloves from a bag she was carrying.

"The idea of planting these trees is that in a few months there will be nutritious and delicious food just hanging around for anyone to eat."

"This is really cool." And I actually started to mean it. It felt good to do something other than shop at a mall. "So, how'd you learn to do all this?"

"Oh well, there are bimonthly training sessions. You just go and they teach you how to get to the distribution center, and they help you get people signed up and organized." She smiled proudly.

"Anyone can do it, really. After today you'll be a superpro. I can tell already. Follow me and I'll introduce you to everyone."

Jana took me over to a group of kids, a few of whom I recognized from Hollis. The group leader put us in charge of digging some holes. I'd never used a shovel, much less dug a hole before.

My first few tries were pathetic; but after I got the hang of it, I was churning up dirt at a rapid pace, and it felt strangely satisfying to be doing something so, well, earthy.

As we prepared to actually plant our first tree, I turned to Jana, a little out of breath. "This is awesome. I've never done anything like this before." She happily scooped the dirt back in to surround the three-foot lemon tree.

"We've got to come back when this thing gets going and pick a few. That'll be so cool."

"Totally."

After a few hours of planting trees, I was exhausted. This was more bodily exertion than I had ever done, even on my most intense shopping day. I needed to refuel. "Why don't we go grab something to eat?" I asked, turning to Jana.

"Sure. I know the perfect place," Jana said, gathering our equipment. We said good-bye to the group and headed to the car. Fifteen minutes later, we had parked and walked into a cute café. We grabbed some menus and sat down.

"That was really great, Jana. Thanks again."

"I guess Newton wasn't big on community service."

"Not really, unless the service you were doing was grabbing a

J. A. Yang

pen and writing a big check. But this was a lot of fun. It felt good to give back to the community."

Jana was about to respond when our waiter appeared. I almost fell off my chair when I looked up into those beautiful green eyes from music class.

"Hey, Jack," Jana said casually.

I smiled, mortified that I was sitting there sweaty, probably smelly, my hair plastered to my face, in cutoffs and a dirty T-shirt. "Uh, hi."

"Hey there, ladies," Jack said, looking at me amusedly. "I see you were doing some gardening today?"

"We went tree planting with my environmental group," Jana replied.

"Sounds fun." He turned to me. "I didn't realize you were environmentally conscious."

"Yup, that's me! Gorgeously green!" I said enthusiastically, smoothing my hair.

"So, what can I get for you?"

Jana and I quickly ordered some lemonade and sandwiches.

"So, what is his story?" I asked as Jack walked away, trying not to sound overly interested.

"I don't know. He doesn't really hang out with anyone I know. But he's really nice, at least whenever I talk to him, which isn't much. And I've never heard anything bad about him. He seems sweet. And he's supercute." She paused and smirked. "Why, are you interested?"

"I don't know. Just curious. He's really gorgeous, and nice, so what's not to like?"

"And he seems to like you. Or at least share your 'curiosity,'" Jana teased.

I couldn't help blushing just a little. I definitely needed to find out more about Jack. The question was, how?

# Chapter
## 10

Monday morning I woke up to the sound of jangling keys. I opened my eyes slowly.

"Hey, sleepyhead. You're running late," Luther said in a sing-song voice as he dangled a set of keys over my head. "But your new ride will save you some time."

"No way. Where'd you get it?" I exclaimed, albeit groggily, and sat up.

"One of my friends had a collection of cars they used on-set for *Herbie Does It Again*. He said we could just have one."

"Ohmigosh, thanks!" I said as I threw on some clothes and rushed outside to examine my new-old ride. Luther followed, practically bursting with excitement.

I ran into the driveway and came to a dead stop next to a gray Honda.

"You like?" Luther asked.

"Umm . . ."

"Look at this; the front bumper has a big dent! It'll be so

authentic as your Lilly-mobile. This is what you wanted, right?"

Looking over the very old car, I was a little worried that this might be too authentic. The whole thing looked a little shaky. As I got into the driver's seat, I looked around for the CD player and realized that none existed. The windows were manual too. "Am I going to get stuck on the side of the road with this thing?"

"Why, hello, Chloe-Grace, can you tell me where Lilly went?" Luther said with a hint of amusement.

Realizing how rude I was being, I quickly backtracked. "Never mind. This will be perfect. Thanks, Luther, you're the best."

"I know," he said, and gave me a hug.

As I arrived at school in my rickety ride, I managed to find a spot in Hollis's beast of a parking lot. Walking what felt like five miles through the main quad, I saw Henry scurrying ahead of me.

"Hey," I said, catching up and tapping him on the shoulder. His entire body twitched as if he'd been shocked, and he stumbled and dropped the books he'd been holding. The heavy geometry one landed right on my open-sandaled toe.

"Ouch," I exclaimed as a reflex.

Wide-eyed, Henry stared first at me and then at his books on the ground. "Omigosh, I'm so sorry. I'm so sorry. I'm so sorry."

My toe still throbbing a little bit, I stooped to help him grab his books. "No, I'm sorry. I probably should have just called your name or something. Here, I have your book for you." I handed him the graphic novel he'd given me last week.

"Did you like it?" he asked, taking the book.

"Yeah, it was really, um, not bad." To be honest, I'd lost interest after a few pages. I tried to get through it, I really did; but some things just weren't meant to be. "How was the movie?"

We finished gathering his stuff and headed inside. "It was really amazing. You should definitely see it," he insisted.

"How did your dad like it?" I said extraloudly, trying to be heard over the din of the early morning hallway chatter.

"Actually, he didn't make it. He had to work." There was something I could definitely relate to.

"What does your dad do?" I asked, intrigued.

"He works at this restaurant."

"Oh, like, he's a chef?"

Henry looked at me strangely. "No. He's a server."

Oh. Somehow I had envisioned my parents being successful businesspeople or something. I took a new look at Henry, dressed today in the same teal-and-white striped sweater and tapered jeans he wore last week. Maybe he just couldn't afford to dress fashionably?

While I was wrapping my mind around this new piece of information, Angela came up beside me. "Lilly! Hey, I heard you went to that tree thing with Jana this weekend."

Noticing Henry for the first time, she said, "Oh, I'm sorry." She then took another careful look at him as he cowered. She looked at me with both eyebrows raised.

"Angela," I said, introducing them, "this is Henry."

"Hey," she said without much enthusiasm.

Henry awkwardly half waved, half nodded, and turned to quickly shuffle away before I could say anything.

"Okay, who is that?" Angela burst into laughter.

Feeling very sisterly, I sprang to my brother's defense. "He's really nice. He's in my geometry class. Don't laugh at him."

She tried to control herself. "He may be nice but, wow, such a dork."

"Fine, he's not that cool. But you can't judge everyone by how they look."

Undaunted, Angela shrugged. "If you say so." As she switched topics and starting telling me about something going on this upcoming weekend and how we had to go, I thought about how hard it must be for my brother. If this was how people reacted to him, how was he ever going to learn to be social? As an older sister, it was my responsibility to show him a few things.

After absentmindedly agreeing to do something or other this weekend, I spent the rest of my morning classes trying to figure out how best to help Henry. By geometry class, I decided I had to come up with some way to hang out with him outside of class.

We paired up again for the homework assignment. We were regular geometry partners now, and when Hannah had kept giving me looks, I'd had to pull her aside and explain that I wanted to partner up with him because he was so good at geometry and that really helped me out. She'd agreed, but still looked at me as if I was crazy to always pair up with him.

As I moved my desk next to Henry's, he looked up from writing in his notebook.

"Hey, do you think you could help me study for the test next week?"

"Wh-what?" he stammered, looking around in minipanic.

"I was thinking we could get together sometime to study. I think I need some help, and you always seem to know how to do everything."

Taking a minute to mull over the statement, he slowly nodded. "Um, okay, I guess."

"Great, so can you do Thursday? We can study at my house after school. Is that cool?"

"Okay. How do I get home from your house? The bus?" he asked meekly.

"Don't worry about it. I'll just drive you."

Not only would this give me a chance to do a minimakeover on Henry, but driving him home would allow me to see where he—where my birth parents—lived. It was a big step, and I was excited to find out more about my family. The question was, could I potentially meet my parents without giving myself away?

On Tuesday I was feeling a little nervous about seeing Jack when I entered the music theater room. I really wanted to talk to him again, but I wasn't sure if he was there or not. He wasn't on Monday. Then halfway through class, he finally appeared, and gave me a little wave from upstairs. When class ended, I purposely lagged behind to wait for him. Just as I was about to give up and head out, he descended the stairs and flashed me a picture-perfect grin.

"You didn't call me this weekend." Skipping right past hello, he picked up right where we had left off last week. He had on a baseball cap today, which covered his curly hair.

"Was I supposed to? Besides, girls don't call boys. You should know that. Plus, you never gave me your number."

"Well, I would have called *you* if I had your number."

"How about you walk me out, and maybe I'll think about giving it to you?" My nervousness melted away. I loved our chemistry, and I'd barely talked to him for more than five minutes.

"Sure." As we walked out of the room, he casually took my backpack and slung it over his shoulder. I didn't mind him being so forward because, hey, when a cute boy carries your books, that's a good thing.

"So, how come you still don't know the words to our esteemed musical selection?"

"Please, I just transferred here last week. I can't sing. And the musical is not my priority. Plus, it's really a safety precaution for everyone involved that I just lip sync."

As we made our way to my locker, I noticed Jack constantly waving or saying bye to people, even as he maintained a conversation with me.

Looking to change the topic, I asked, "Why does it seem like you know everybody here? Am I walking around with Mr. Popularity or what?"

Jack shrugged and laughed. "Hardly. You know that coffee

shop I work at. Well, a lot of people come by, so I'm like their coffee hookup. They're just greeting their server."

Reaching my locker, I was surprised when Jack went directly to a locker near me. "Your locker is right there? How come I've never seen you here before?"

"Well, that's probably because I never come here except to pick this up." From the depths of his locker he pulled out a black guitar case plastered with stickers. I recognized the logos for The Strokes, The Kleptones, and the Chili Peppers.

"That's all you have in there? A guitar?" I raised a suspicious eyebrow.

He took a step back, pretending like I had stabbed him in the heart. "This is not just a guitar. This is my baby and best friend. Lilly, meet Michelle. You're going to have to apologize. She's hurt."

I laughed. "I'm sorry, Michelle." I finished grabbing my things and went over and peered into his locker. "Wow, there's seriously nothing in here. Where do you keep your school stuff?"

"In my car. I'd rather have this close to me than, you know, a bunch of books."

"So, are you any good with that thing?"

"Well, I'm no John Mayer, but I'm not bad." As we walked out to the parking lot, Jack told me about his previous summer spent being a roadie with a local band, The Coolest Ones.

"They said that if I ever got anything serious together they'd help me get some gigs." He said this so enthusiastically and earnestly that I didn't want to say that I had never even heard of the band.

"So, this is something you want to do professionally?" I asked.

"That would be the dream, I guess. Travel the world playing music every step of the way."

I couldn't really help but think of my adoptive dad. I wonder if he'd been this idealistic once.

We reached my new-old car. "So, when am I going to hear you play something?" I asked coyly.

Jack crouched down and opened his guitar case, revealing a vintage Martin nestled inside. "Actually, here's a CD I recorded a while back. It's a bit rough." He handed over a clear plastic case he had taken out of a side pocket.

I took the CD from him. "Nice Martin."

Jack looked up in surprise. "Oh, you know something about guitars?"

Typical. Guys never think girls know anything about instruments, cars, video games, or sports. They're so easily impressed when you do. It's hard not to pick up a few terms when your dad is/was a big star. But Jack didn't have to know that.

"No, not really. I mean, I don't play or anything. I just love hearing the guitar."

"Okay, well, if you like what you hear on the CD, I host an open mike every Wednesday night at the coffee shop. You should come."

"Yeah?" Quite frankly, I wouldn't have cared if his music sounded like nails on a chalkboard. Without even hearing it, I was ready to say that it was great and that I would love to hear some more. But I didn't want to sound overeager. "Sounds fun. I'll try to make it sometime. I'll see you tomorrow, Jack." I gave him my biggest smile and got in the car.

I drove home practically floating on air and rushed to my room to rip Jack's CD onto my iPod. As it was processing, Rachelle pinged me on instant messenger.

RachelleSays: Ms. C, where have you been? You haven't called me!

AstraStar: Hello, I'm overseas. I can't call you.

RachelleSays: Fine. So what's going on over there? What time is it?

AstraStar: It's like really late at night. What've you been doing?

RachelleSays: Oh, you know, since you left everything's fallen apart. School's a bore, I'm dying of jealousy you're away, and my best friend won't tell me what exciting things she's up to.

AstraStar: Well, guess what? I met a guy today!

I was really excited to tell Rachelle about Jack, but I had to talk about him as if he was an entirely different person.

RachelleSays: I knew it! A totally hot Italian guy? What's his name?

AstraStar: Allessandro. He's totally cool and supernice.

RachelleSays: Is he cute?

AstraStar: Very.

In my retelling, Jack, now Allessandro, had been transformed into a twenty-year-old production assistant on my mom's set. I tried to work in the little I knew about him by saying that he was a musician. I e-mailed Rachelle a few of Jack's songs so that we could listen to them at the same time.

AstraStar: Not bad right?

RachelleSays: I like his voice. It sounds like he's really cute. You're going to send me pictures right?

AstraStar: Of course. We haven't even hung out yet but I think we will soon. You try to stay out of trouble without me, k?

RachelleSays: I'll do what I can. Write me!

AstraStar: Nite Rach, miss you!

*AstraStar has signed off.*

I spent the rest of the night listening to Jack's CD. It was only three tracks, but I kept it on major repeat. Jack's music turned out to be quite good—sort of John Mayer/Jack Johnson-esque. His voice was unexpectedly scratchy on his vocals, and it made him sound really, well, sexy. I wondered if he wrote his own lyrics, since they seemed to reveal a thoughtful tender side.

I sunk into my bed and imagined his show, live. I shut my eyes and drifted off, his voice playing through my head.

The next day at lunch, realizing that I didn't want to show up at Jack's open mike alone, I asked the girls what they were doing that night.

"You know, the usual," Jana said. "Studying. It's a weeknight."

"Why? You've got something for us to do?" Angela asked, curious.

"Well, I was thinking that maybe you guys would want to go to an open mike thing with me tonight."

Stefanie looked intrigued. "Where's this open mike?"

"It's at Café B, the one we went to, Jana. Jack invited me."

"Did he now?" Jana said, smirking. "I've heard him play before. He's pretty good. He should be famous."

"You guys would make such a cute couple," Stefanie added out of nowhere.

"Just think, if he became a famous musician, you'd be famous too."

I smiled wanly, trying not to cringe. "We're not even together. . . ."

"Speaking of famous," Angela jumped in, "I was just telling my mom the other day that you reminded me of someone." She squinted her eyes, examining me. "Chloe-Grace Star. You kind of look like her. Like you have the same big eyes and cute, pointy chin. You know?"

My heart froze, and I didn't know what to do. I felt suddenly sick. Nobody had questioned my Lilly identity since I'd been here, and I'd felt so safe the past two and a half weeks.

"Angela! That's so not true. They're just both Chinese. Not all Chinese people look the same!" Jana said. "Next you're gonna say Lilly looks like Lucy Liu, right?"

Despite being reprimanded, Angela didn't back off. She reached into her bag and took out an issue of *Fame* magazine. "Look, let me show you this picture."

As she flipped through the pages, I started to panic.

"Well, that's really flattering, Angela, but you know, that's just hilarious—me looking like somebody famous." I did my best to seem nonchalant about the whole thing.

Finally finding the picture she was looking for, Angela stopped and flipped the magazine around to show the rest of us. "Look," she said, pointing a finger at a picture of Rachelle and me from last year. "You guys don't think they look the same here?"

While Stefanie and Jana leaned in for a closer look, Angela flagged down Brett from the table next to us. "Brett, come here. Doesn't Lilly look like Chloe-Grace Star?"

He studied the photo closely and then examined me. "Well, no offense, Lilly, but not really. Sorry, Angela."

I felt relieved, even if Brett had implied that Chloe and Lilly were light-years apart in the looks department. Whatever, as long as they didn't know we were one and the same.

"Man, I'd like to get a better look at this chick, though. Who's she?" Brett took hold of the magazine for a closer look.

"That's Rachelle Torres. She's, like, our age," Angela said.

"Damn, she's our age? Why don't any of you girls look like her? Man, she's hot!"

All the girls groaned. "Get out of here!"

Brett took one last look before leaving while Angela turned back to the picture of Rachelle and sighed deeply. "She *is* superhot, though. Her clothes are so amazing. I wonder how she looks so grown-up like that."

I felt as if I had to say something. "Well, I'm sure she spends her whole day dressing up or something. It takes a lot of work to do that. Nobody's naturally that beautiful." This was an outright lie, of course, because Rachelle *was* that naturally beautiful, but I wanted Angela to see how pretty she was too. "I mean, c'mon, Angela, I'm sure if you had all that stuff done to you, you'd look ten times hotter than her."

She smiled. "I don't believe you for a second, but thanks for saying it."

As lunch ended, the girls agreed to meet me and go to Jack's open mike later that night. I was looking forward to it, but it was still unsettling that Angela had made the connection between me and Chloe. I just hoped it ended there.

Café B turned out to be really small and cozy at night—a different atmosphere than the one I remembered during my first visit there. Some tables had been moved, replaced with a small stage and comfortable but unmatched couches haphazardly thrown together. Natural light was replaced with elegant tea lights and candles.

Dressed in a Café B polo shirt with a white apron folded down at the waist, Jack was busy behind the counter when we walked in. He looked up and smiled. "Lilly, you came!"

"Of course, wouldn't miss it for the world." I flashed him my brightest smile. "And I brought some friends. You know Jana. And this is Angela and Stefanie."

"I'm really glad you came out. Can I make you guys anything? It's on the house." He looked at me and winked. He was getting cuter by the minute, and he hadn't even started playing any music yet! The four of us ordered coffee and then sat down at a round table right in front of the small stage.

"Lilly, he is so totally into you. He keeps looking over here," Jana whispered to me.

"Yeah, he has that problem." I smirked. "He told me that he's been watching me during music class. He mans the spotlights, and he can just stare without repercussions. It's really embarrassing." I blushed.

Stefanie kept studying him. "Yup, his eyes haven't left you yet. Trust me, I'm watching. You guys would be adorable together. I hate you already," she said with a smile.

Jack brought over our drinks and then headed back to work. Meanwhile, the open mike night started. Currently onstage was a sad-looking girl playing the keyboard and singing in a high-pitched falsetto. She really wasn't that good—although way better than me—but I clapped loudly anyway because I wanted Jack to know that I could appreciate an artist, any artist. During her third eardrum-bursting song, I took my coffee up to the counter and pretended to pour some more sugar into it. Then I walked over to Jack and leaned gently against the counter, with my back to him, as if I was listening intently to her song.

I felt Jack's warm breath near my neck as he leaned in. "Sorry about this. Sometimes the performances are a little bit, um, hard to sit through."

"Oh, it's okay. I don't mind. I mean, we don't mind." I turned around to face him. "When are you going to go on?"

"Well, I wait until there's nobody left, so it'll probably be after those guys in the corner. They usually go last."

"So they're like your opening act, right?"

Jack smiled wide and said, "Something like that. I never thought about it that way."

"Well, I'm here to request an encore."

"You can't do that. I haven't even gone yet," he said, his lips really close to mine.

"Well, that's not fair," I said teasingly. "I can't ask you for one extra song? You're not going to make me give you a standing ovation, are you?"

He laughed. "Fine, I'll see what I can do. If nobody boos me off the stage, that is."

"I'll try to keep the booing to a minimum." And with that I dramatically turned away from him and headed back to my seat.

After we sat through twenty minutes of the grunge guys rock and violin combo, Jack finally took the stage. Hearing his music live, with him sitting there and playing right in front of me, was so much more amazing than his CD. Even with his songs stripped down to just his voice and a guitar, I thought his music was really, really good.

Near the end of his second song, Stefanie nudged my elbow. "How do you know all the words to his stuff?"

I hadn't even noticed I'd been singing along to his lyrics, hopefully very quietly. I shrugged and turned back to Jack. My cheeks turned red, and I sort of hoped Jack hadn't noticed. What kind of crazy girl memorizes all of your lyrics overnight?

As he played, Jack turned out toward the audience and continually made eye contact with just about everyone but me. I guess I couldn't expect him to just look at me like it was a private concert. As he finished his third and final song, Jack stood up from the stool, readjusted his guitar strap, and raised the mike stand. "Usually I'd stop here to spare you guys, but I've had a special request for an encore. So if you please, could everyone stand up as I sing this for a special someone?"

The crowd eagerly rose to their feet. With a smile in my direction, Jack started playing. A few notes in, even before he started singing, I recognized the song. Of all the songs in the entire history of music, he had chosen to cover my dad's band's one-hit romantic wonder. My mouth dropped open in shock.

By the end of the first verse, Jack was no longer looking out at the audience as a whole. He looked squarely in my direction the entire time. I felt hot, and my skin got all goose pimply.

Jack finished his song, and while everyone gave him a round of applause, I couldn't even clap, I was so astonished. Nobody had ever done that before, like done something so publicly romantic for me. Unless you counted Austin ramming his tongue down my throat at the Lakers game as romantic. This was the direct opposite of that. And while it was my dad's song, which made this whole thing incredibly weird, Jack had dedicated a song to me. No wonder my mom fell for my dad.

Jack broke out into a suddenly sheepish smile and said into

the mike, "Thank you, everyone, come back next week. Good night!"

With guitar still in hand, he came directly over to us and did a little theatrical flourish with his arm as we gave him another round of applause.

"That was great," Stefanie gushed.

"I'm really glad you guys came," he said. "If you don't mind sticking around, I'll close up shop and then we can hang out in here for a while? Maybe some cake or dessert? Anything you want."

His question hung in the air, as we weren't exactly sure what to do. I darted a look at the girls, but they waited for me to answer. "Sure, that sounds great," I replied after the slight pause.

"Great, let me get everything cleaned up. I'll be right back."

Jack stood up and went into the back. Most of the other customers were already on their way out the door as we remained at our table.

"Do you want us to leave you two alone Lilly?" Jana asked. Angela and Stefanie giggled. I did really want to hang out with Jack but didn't want to ditch the girls, because they had been nice enough to come with me.

"No, I want you guys to stay. It's totally cool. Please." I thought it would be a better way to get to know Jack, to see how he interacted with my friends.

He emerged from the back with a work apron slung over his shoulder. He went behind the counter to pour us more coffee and then brought the mugs and a cake to our table.

"I hope you guys like carrot cake. This stuff is seriously the best in the city," he said, laying out four forks. As Jack returned to sweeping and cleaning up, we each took a bite and decided that he was absolutely right.

"He's cute, he sings, he brings cake. There's got to be something wrong with him." Jana laughed.

In the afterglow of Jack's performance, I had this blinding moment of intense happiness. Here I was, sitting in a totally charming coffee shop with good friends, a cute guy had just sung directly to me, and nobody was trailing me trying to get the scoop. Life seemed so natural and easy this way, without pressure, worries, or the vile specter of the paparazzi. I wondered how long I could live in disguise. Part of me hoped that it might be forever.

We finished our cake, and Jack walked out with us and locked up. As we headed toward the parking lot, Jana turned to him. "Hey, could you take Lilly home for us? She's on your way, right?"

Taking only a moment to follow her train of thought, he said, "That's fine with me, if Lilly's okay with it."

I hoped my sudden blush didn't show and of course readily agreed.

"Oh well, maybe you can drop me off too then? I'm, like, right there," Stefanie added. Angela gave her a quick elbow. "Oh, I mean, um, never mind. We'll be fine. Have fun, guys." The three of them giggled as they left.

On our way home in Jack's pickup truck, he asked, "So, what do you say we do something this weekend, maybe just you and me?" He quickly amended, "Not that your friends aren't great, but it would be nice to have a chance to just hang out together alone. Do you like the beach?"

"I love the beach. That would be awesome."

"How do you feel about surfing? If you're free sometime, we could maybe do that?"

I didn't know how to surf at all. Most of the time, the beach meant wearing a supercute bikini and laying out to get the perfect tan. But here's to new things, right?

"That sounds great. If you can live with me falling all over the place."

"Oh, I think I can manage."

He pulled up to Luther's house, and I swear I saw Luther's shadow in the window. I smiled and rolled my eyes.

"So, I'll see you tomorrow. Thanks again for coming out tonight."

"Thank you for . . . everything. It was a lot of fun," I said, smiling into his eyes.

After a momentary pause, he leaned over and kissed me on the cheek, taking my breath away with the suddenness of his movements.

"My pleasure."

I sat with a silly grin on my face, finally realizing after a moment that I needed to get out of his truck. I opened the door, said one last good night, then practically skipped up the steps as he pulled away.

After classes on Thursday I waited in the parking lot for Henry to show up for our study session. Fifteen minutes after school let out, there was still no sign of him. Finally, I saw him emerge from the entrance, and I waved to him. "Hey, what took so long?" I asked as he approached.

Looking sheepish, he said, "Sorry, I had to call my mom. She wanted to know when to pick me up. I didn't know what to say."

"I'll just bring you home after we're done, remember. It's no big deal."

"Okay, but I have to be home before dinner, though."

"No problem." I unlocked the door and indicated for him to get in.

As I drove to Luther's, I made small talk and asked him what he did during lunches at school. "I never see you around."

"Oh, I hang out in the computer lab."

"The computer lab? I didn't even realize you could eat lunch in there."

"I'm part of the computer club. I play games. With my friends."

"Lemme guess, they're all guys?" I didn't even wait for him to answer before offering him a suggestion. "Maybe one of these days you can come eat lunch with me and my friends? They're all really nice, and I think it'll be good for you. How's that sound?"

He thought about it a moment and then answered, "Scary."

I laughed at him. "I promise you they aren't. Okay?"

"Um, maybe?" He seemed hesitant, but I promised myself that I'd just drag him to lunch with us one day.

"Wow, you live here?" he asked as we pulled up to Luther's house. "This is really nice."

I wasn't sure if he was kidding, because Luther's house was actually just a small town house. It seemed pretty ordinary to me. In fact, since Luther spent so much time at his workshop, this was really his secondary residence and not overly impressive, especially from the outside.

Once we actually got inside, the ultramodern and minimalist decor that Luther loved made Henry gawk even more. "I've never seen a house like this. I can't believe you live here. It looks like a furniture store. This is seriously cool."

"You can put your bag down." He had been clutching it to his chest, afraid to set it down anywhere. "C'mon, we'll use this table to study on." I settled us in Luther's living room and spread out my books on his granite-top table.

Soon afterward we were engrossed in doing old homework sets, and Henry was extremely helpful in patiently walking me through a few tricky problems.

Enveloped in our studying, neither of us noticed Luther coming in until he exclaimed, "Lilly! Who is this ragamuffin you've dragged in here?" He was teasing, of course, but Henry's face turned sheet white.

Sensing his panic, I quickly said, "This is Henry from school, and this is Luther, my . . ."

"Friend," I said.

"Dad," Luther said.

I don't know what made me say that Luther wasn't my dad;

but I guess with Henry around, I subconsciously just strayed away from introducing Luther as family.

Henry looked really confused.

Recovering faster than I could, Luther let out a chuckle. "What she means is that I'm so cool that I'm really more like her friend than her dad. But let me assure you, I am her dad." Having neatly diffused the situation, Luther glided over to shake Henry's hand.

"Well, aren't you just the cutest thing, going retro-geek." Luther said this with a perfectly straight face. "It's really a popular look right now. Where did you find the authentic pieces?"

I cringed at the misunderstanding but couldn't help being really amused. Henry was so earnest and off balanced that he squeaked out, "This is just stuff I've always had. You really think it's cool?" He looked down at his faded Billabong T-shirt, seeing everything in a new light.

Ignoring his question, Luther turned his attention to Henry's classic bowl-cut haircut. "And this is really the pièce de résistance. Lilly, where did you find this boy?" Luther asked, turning to me.

"Geometry class. We're studying for a big test tomorrow. Hey, um, Dad, could I talk to you for a second?" I was suddenly fearful of where Luther would take the conversation next.

"Of course, honey. You just sit tight, Henry; we'll be right back."

I led Luther into the kitchen and shut the door. "Luther! He doesn't mean to dress that way. It's not a style thing."

"Shut up!" he exclaimed, putting his hand over his mouth.

"You mean he's not doing that on purpose? Oh, how tragic. So, what is he doing here?"

"I told you, we're studying for a geometry test tomorrow."

"You're great at math. You don't need help. And he's hardly someone you'd date." He paused and studied me closely. "What's really going on here?"

I didn't know what to say. Any lie I came up with Luther would see right through. I took a deep breath and made the decision to launch into the whole explanation, albeit the abbreviated version. "You can keep a secret, right? And promise not to tell my mom?"

Luther looked really intrigued now.

"Okay. Long story short, he's my brother. Like my real biological brother." I waited for that to sink in.

Luther's eyes got really big. I hastily put my hand over his mouth to prevent any verbal explosions. "Shhh, I didn't tell you the whole reason I transferred. But I came to Hollis because Jean-Paul helped me find my biological parents, and I found out that my parents were living in Alhambra and that I had a little brother in high school here. That's part of why I transferred. I'm sorry for keeping it from you."

I hadn't thought about when I would let Luther in on my entire plan, but now that I'd been in school here almost two weeks and things were clearly progressing on the finding-the-family front, it felt as if I shouldn't keep it from him anymore.

Luther looked as if I'd just told him an underage Disney starlet was pregnant. "I can't believe that is your brother. You guys don't look anything alike. Well, you're both Asian, I guess. Ohmigosh, does he *know*?"

Wishing Luther didn't talk so loud, I whispered urgently, "Of course not. I haven't told him yet. I'm just trying to be friends with him so that I can . . ." I trailed off, not sure exactly what I was trying to do.

"You're trying to establish a life away from your family. Wow. You certainly are full of surprises, Chloe-Grace."

"You won't tell my mom, right? Please. I know you tell her everything but this is really important to me. I don't want her to find out until I'm ready."

"I can do that. The roommate bond is more important than ten years of friendship and a steady paycheck anyway, right?" This time I couldn't stop Luther's high-pitched laugh from ringing throughout the house.

Not wanting to keep Henry waiting too long and surely confusing him thoroughly by now, I quickly said, "I'll tell you all the details later, okay? I was just hoping that by bringing him over we could give him a makeover or something. He's, like, so geeky."

"You're right. We can't have that in the family. There was something way too authentic about his geekiness. Less geek chic, more weak geek. Don't worry about it. I'll take care of everything."

Without waiting for a response, Luther pulled the door aside and burst through. I followed him into the living room. "Alright, young man, today's your lucky day. After a bit of discussion, we've decided that your look isn't as fashion forward as I'd initially thought. Lilly and I want to give you a complete make-over; what do you think?"

Luther's dad-voice had completely slipped away, but Henry didn't seem to be bothered by that. Instead, he just sat there staring at the both of us.

I gave him a supportive smile. "My dad's a fashion stylist; he'll totally make you cool."

"I'm not sure what you mean by 'makeover'?" Henry said.

"We'll take this incredible look you have going here and just make it so much better. Seriously, you'll love it. I can do wonders with you." Luther looked at me meaningfully.

Luther took Henry straightaway to the bathroom and said that they were going to start with a haircut. As I stood in the doorway to watch, he ushered me away. "Hair cutting is such a private thing. Let me take care of him. Don't worry about a thing."

With that, I went back to study some more geometry.

Forty minutes later, Luther came in and announced, "Are you ready?"

Looking up from my books eagerly, I said, "Yes!"

"Introducing the new-and-improved Henry." With a dramatic flourish, Luther waved Henry in, and I almost dropped out of my seat in shock. His entirely unfashionable bowl cut had been cropped into a short and spiky do that made him look as if he was finally out of middle school. He even seemed to stand up straighter because of it.

He smiled. "Pretty cool, huh?"

"Yeah, do you love it?"

"I think I do," he said.

After his new haircut and a promise from Luther to get him some new clothes to try on next time he came over, Henry had to go. As we drove to his house, he kept chattering about how cool Luther was. Lost in all his excitement was the fact that I was taking my little brother home to our parents. I didn't know what to expect.

The first surprise was that my parents didn't live in a house at all. As we drove around the condos where they lived, I went through the community really slowly, pretending to carefully look at the numbers on the buildings. I was appalled at how run-down and small everything seemed.

The shock of knowing that my birth parents didn't even own a house, like a real house, took me out of any fantasy I had about their wonderful American life. It made me so sad that I momentarily teared up. Luckily, Henry wasn't paying attention as I quickly dabbed at my eyes.

"It's right there, next to that one," Henry directed, pointing up to the right.

I pulled over and fought the urge to ask Henry if his parents were home. As I hesitated to say good-bye as he got out of the car, he stopped short of closing the door. "Uh, did you want to come in? Like, do you need to use the bathroom or something?"

Shaken out of my thoughts, I couldn't answer him even as he stood there waiting. Did I want to come in? That question captured everything I had been trying to figure out since I'd decided to leave Newton. It would be so easy just to go in, see who my parents were, and then tell them who I was. Or maybe they would recognize me? Would that be better or worse than if they didn't?

I wasn't ready for this. No way. "No, I'm fine. I'll see you tomorrow," I replied, disappointed in myself.

"Okay, have a good night! Thanks again so much!" And with that he slammed the car door and ran away with his bag slapping against his legs. I watched him as he rounded the corner and disappeared out of sight.

Immediately after pulling out of his complex, I called Vickie on my cell. I tried to keep my voice from wavering to balance out how distraught I felt.

"I couldn't do it Vick," I said shakily.

"Chloe! What's wrong? What couldn't you do?" Vickie sounded immediately concerned.

"I just dropped Henry off at his house, and he asked if I wanted to come up. I wanted to, I really did. But I couldn't. I just wasn't ready."

"What do you mean? I thought this is what your plan was all along?"

"I know, but I froze. I saw their house, well, it's not even a house. I felt really guilty. Like, I felt so, I dunno, privileged? Maybe that's the word? Like I'd gotten this whole amazing crazy life that they didn't."

Vickie took a long time to say anything while I kept rambling. "Chloe, stop. It's not like this is something that you should feel bad about. It's not your fault. This isn't anything you did."

But it felt that way even if it was totally irrational. They had put me up for adoption, not the other way around. It just seemed so wrong that I'd been dropped into this huge life and they, well, they weren't.

"Take your time figuring out exactly how you want everything to work out. There's no rush at all. You know? Listen to yourself! Less than a month ago you were dying to get out of your crazy life. Remember? You wanted to see what it would be like to be normal. Maybe it's better? It doesn't matter how you live, Chloe."

As always, what Vickie said made so much sense. I'd been having a great time at Hollis, and just being faced with the option of seeing my birth parents didn't mean I had to if I wasn't ready. I resolved to take it slow and wait for the perfect moment to tell them about me. For now I'd just do my best to be a good friend to everyone, and a secret sister to Henry. That wouldn't be too overwhelming, right?

# Chapter
## 11

Friday afternoon, after I easily aced the geometry test that I didn't really need Henry's help studying for, Jana and I headed over to the bookstore to browse through magazines.

"So, have you talked to Jack after his open mike night?" Jana asked, flipping through *Environment Today* magazine.

"Here and there, but he's been so busy with work. He does want to take me out, though. We have a date tomorrow."

"Ooh, an official first date."

"Mmhmm." I smiled and picked up *Vogue*.

"Um, looks like you've got another admirer—though this one's a little creepy," Jana said, indicating where with a slight tilt of her head.

Looking up from my issue of *Vogue*, I made brief eye contact with a middle-aged man standing two aisles away. He was a bit paunchy and not very tall, and was dressed in a bad polo shirt and khakis. Once he realized that I'd caught him looking, he averted his eyes and quickly headed toward the door.

"What was he doing?" I asked, watching him leave the store.

"I'm pretty sure he was taking camera-phone pictures of you. I saw him holding his phone up in your direction. And that was after he kept staring at you. It was really weird."

"How long was he there?" I asked, trying to steady my panicky voice.

"I dunno. I just turned around, and I saw him pointing his phone at you. He must have thought you were really cute."

God, I hoped that was it. I worried that it might have been more than that. Did he take a picture of me because he thought he recognized Chloe-Grace? There was no way, right? It'd been such an awesome two weeks of not having to worry about paparazzi or anyone following me around that I couldn't decide if I was overreacting or not.

Shortly after, I dropped Jana off at her house. Once I got back to Luther's, I found him sitting on the couch watching a *Project Model* rerun.

"Look at this girl, Chloe. She should not be on this show at all. It's terrible how horrific she walks. She sways side to side like a hippo and thinks it's runway worthy. I have got to get on one of these shows as a judge. It's just too easy!"

"I think you deserve your own show, actually."

"Well, aren't you a doll. That's a great suggestion." Turning down the volume on the TV, he narrowed his eyes at me suspiciously. "You look kind of frazzled. What's going on?"

"Today, at the bookstore, I might have had a close encounter with a stalker or something. But I can't figure out if it was because he actually thought I was Chloe, or if he was just some weird guy taking a picture of a girl."

"So you're thinking the disguise isn't working," Luther said.

"I'm not sure. It wasn't a problem at all until today." Stopping to think about it some more, I added, "Actually, at lunch earlier this week someone mentioned how similar I looked to Chloe-Grace."

"You have to know this won't last forever, Chloe. Eventually someone's going to find out what you're doing or who you really are. I can make you look different but not invisible."

"But, Luther, it's only been two weeks!"

"Maybe you should consider going to Capri for the weekend. Join your mother and show your face a little. Show that Chloe-Grace is actually in Capri. You can wear a wig and dress in your designer clothes again. Sooner or later, people will start wondering where you are."

He had a point there. It wouldn't be possible for me just to disappear completely. "Maybe you're right, Luther. I'll think about it."

In the meantime, I resolved to enjoy my anonymity while I had it. I chalked up today's bookstore experience to just some weird old guy and left it at that.

With my new attitude in mind, I vowed not to spend the entire next day with Jack—my first official date!—worrying about who might be looking over my shoulder. I didn't care anymore; I just wanted to have fun.

Jack picked me up early Saturday afternoon in his beat-up pickup truck, two surfboards dangling haphazardly out of the back. I felt a little ashamed that I was so pale (I'd run out of time for a fake bake) compared to his dark tan and had considered wearing a one-piece. However, I decided that a one-piece would just send the wrong, unsexy message and tied on a bikini top and slipped on board shorts instead.

The sun was shining bright and the sky was decorated with wispy clouds. Perfect weather for a perfect date. Even though it was only April, Jack assured me that the water was warm enough for a surfing lesson. Just in case, he had brought a half suit for each of us.

As we zipped along the freeway with the windows down and my short hair whipping around my face, I took the opportunity to ask him, "So, do you do this a lot?"

Smiling a bit, he adjusted his wraparound sunglasses. "If you mean surfing, then, yes. If you mean do I get the chance to take a cute girl to the beach often, then, no."

"This isn't your usual first-date thing, then?" I said, smirking. I realized that I actually didn't know anything about his relationship history. I thought it best if I got some basic information, you know, for research purposes.

"Naw, this is just for fun. Maybe what we're doing afterward might be a date, though."

"What have you got planned afterward?" I wanted to know.

"I was thinking an afternoon picnic? I already packed everything." He indicated the back of the truck. I looked over and saw an actual wicker picnic basket tucked underneath the surfboards. This was amazing. What had I done to deserve this? I can't remember ever going on a romantic picnic—and certainly not with Austin. I was glad I had opted for the bikini.

When we arrived at Huntington Beach, Jack picked a spot for us on the sand and laid out a few towels. Taking off his shirt to reveal a lean and muscular torso, he grinned. "Ready to start?"

"Sure, what do I do? Just grab this thing and go running in?" I looked at the smaller of the two surfboards. "This one's for me?"

Laughing, he picked up the board that seemed to be twice my height. "Actually, this one is. It's easier to learn on a long board. C'mon, I'll teach you a few basics and then we'll go out."

Tethering the board leash to my right ankle, he carried my board into the water and waited for me to follow. As I gingerly dipped in my feet, the water turned out to be screechingly cold. "Jack! You said the water would be warm!"

"It's just cold at first. You'll get used to it when you start moving around." He warned, "Don't make me splash you!"

I glared menacingly at him. "You wouldn't dare!" But before he could answer, I scooped a cup of water into my hand and flung it at him. He let out a yelp, and I couldn't help laughing. Before he could splash me back, I ran straight toward an incoming small wave and crashed through it. I emerged shivering from the icy cold.

"C'mon, turtle, you're slowing me down!" I playfully tugged at the leash on my ankle. He high stepped his way through the water and chased after me.

We spent the next thirty minutes engaged in surfing practice.

I actually sort of stood up once as Jack lent me a hand to maintain my balance. I glided all the way into shore until I hopped off and turned to give him a dramatic bow.

"That was amazing! You're a total natural!" Jack said, thrilled and excited.

Unstrapping the surfboard and leaving it on the beach, I ran up to him. "I think I just have a really great teacher."

He looked at me and leaned in and kissed me. The combination of his warm lips and the cold salt water was exhilarating, and I didn't feel anything except a tingling sensation all over my body.

As we pulled apart and sat down on our towels, I nestled into his chest. We watched the waves crashing on the sand, and at this moment I didn't think anything could be more perfect.

On Tuesday (after a blissful all-Jack weekend!), I purposely set out to drag Henry with me to eat lunch. I'd already helped out his look; now the next sisterly thing to do was to help his social situation. Plus, if I was going to eventually reveal that Henry was my brother, I wanted him to get along with my friends.

Now that I knew where he was holed up, I headed directly to the computer lab. Gingerly opening the door, I peeked in. Two boys were sitting at computers, each in an opposite corner. I saw the top of Henry's newly coiffed head bobbing up above one of the screens farthest from the door. There was no teacher in sight.

I walked over to Henry and looked at his screen. Dozens of

little monsters ran around as he expertly moved his mouse with his right hand. Waiting until it seemed as if there was a lull, I gently tapped him on the head, and he jumped a little, as usual. Lifting his headphones off his ears, he turned around.

"Lilly?"

"Hi, wh—"

"Hey, why'd you stop?" His friend across the room stood up to see what was going on. Supertall and thin in his oversize tee, he was wearing a frighteningly thick pair of glasses, which made his eyes seem inhumanly large as he saw me and stared, bug-eyed. I gave him a little wave.

Taking that as a sign to come over, he walked up to us. "Hey, I'm Bobby. Who're you?"

"She's in my geometry class. We're partners," Henry announced. He sounded really proud. Bobby looked at me and said, "Oh, are you guys doing homework or something?"

"Not really, I just wanted to see exactly what it was Henry did in here. What are you guys playing?"

"Um, Battlecraft," Henry said.

"Right. So, are you almost done?"

"We just started, actually." He looked at Bobby and shrugged.

"How about you stop right now and let's go eat," I offered.

Henry made no move to get up. "C'mon, this'll be good for you. Let's go. Seriously. Bobby, you can come too."

"Well, uh, okay . . ." Henry shut down his computer and took his bag as Bobby gathered his stuff. The two of them trailed after me into the lunchroom. They looked as if they'd never set foot in the place before, and I had to practically pull them in with me.

"Okay, we're going to sit with my friends. Don't be intimidated. They're supernice. Just talk to them."

"I don't know what to say," Henry said.

"Well, ask some questions."

"Like what?" they said in unison.

"Like anything." I wondered if maybe I should have prepped them with some prequestions. Maybe even given them something on index cards, like a How to Be Social cheat sheet.

"Okay, not anything. Maybe try asking what grade they're in. Where they live. Don't worry, I'll make it easy for you."

Looking extremely doubtful, they both just dutifully followed me across the room to where Jana, Angela, and Stefanie were sitting.

"Hey, guys, this is Henry and Bobby. Henry's in my geometry class. They're going to eat with us today."

All three of the girls raised their eyebrows at me and gave me "Who are these guys?" looks.

Jana, always dependably sweet, was the first to speak. "Hey, guys. Here, we'll slide over."

I ushered them into their seats and did my best to engage them in conversation. The problem was, they weren't very responsive. Angela and Stefanie soon lost interest and started chatting by themselves. Jana and I plugged on.

"So, are you guys best friends?" Jana asked, clearly trying to help.

They looked at each other and shrugged. "Yeah," said Henry. "We've known each other since fifth grade."

"That's cool. How're you guys liking high school?" Jana was trying her best, but we couldn't get any conversation going. I was starting to think this was a terrible idea.

"Umm, it's okay, I guess," Bobby said.

Fine, this was officially a mistake. After running out of small talk, we all sat eating, listening to ourselves chew our food. It was becoming almost unbearable until I felt a light hand on my neck. I turned around, and Jack leaned in to give me a light kiss on the cheek. Both Angela and Stefanie raised their eyebrows in excitement, and Jana smiled knowingly.

"Hey, guys, mind if I sit here?"

"Of course not," Angela singsonged.

We made space for him. He ended up sitting next to me and across from Henry and Bobby.

"So, who's this?" he asked.

"This is Henry and Bobby. Henry's helping me in Mr. Ramirez's geometry class."

Being superpersonable, Jack soon got them talking. It was amazing. As it turned out, Jack was quite the video game aficionado himself and was able to get them all excited talking about Battlecraft.

Turning to the girls, I half whispered, "Hey, sorry about that. I probably should have asked you guys beforehand. Henry's really, well, socially awkward, so I'm trying to help him out since he's really helped me in class."

Wrinkling her nose, Angela said, "Wow, you *are* as big of a humanitarian as Jana."

"Bigger maybe," Stefanie said as she threw a meaningful look at the boys.

I looked again as Jack animatedly talked to Henry and Bobby. I couldn't help but think that he was being great with my brother, not only my geometry partner.

At the end of lunch I walked out with Jack.

"So, I'm just trying to help Henry be more social. He's been really great in class, helping me study. I thought I'd return the favor, even though I wasn't really asked."

"That's very sweet of you. It's almost like you're a big sister to him."

I smiled. *Actually* . . .

"And thank you for being so great with them. You totally saved what would have been an incredibly awkward lunch."

"No problem. They're capable of talking to people. You just have to help them out a little."

"Easy for you to say. You're a total natural," I teased. "Oh, by the way, how do you know so much about video games?"

"You think I got that good at video games by *not* being a dork at some point in my life? I was just like those two as a freshman." Looking over at Bobby and Henry dropping their books as they ran to class, he continued, "Okay, maybe not exactly."

We both laughed.

"Anyway, I'd better get going. I'll see you later."

And with that he leaned over and kissed me quickly, and headed down the hall.

As I walked to class I thought about what Luther had said. Maybe I could continue this normal life and no one would know. Things seemed to get better every day. Jack was amazing, Henry was adorably sweet, I had great friends.

I just couldn't see any of this ending—ever.

# Chapter
## 12

Striding up to me purposefully during lunch on Friday, Angela had a crazed look in her eyes. The boys hadn't shown up yet, but Jack, Stefanie, and Jana were already eating.

Angela half shoved a magazine into my hands. "Ohmigod, look at this! It's incredible."

I took the magazine, and my smile quickly disappeared. At that moment my entire perfect world came crashing down on me. It was a gossip rag, of course. The magazine was turned to an article, one with a picture of me with short hair. The headline read: "You won't believe where she's been!"

"Where did you get this?" I moaned as panic alarms went off in my head.

"At the newspaper stand this morning. It's the newest issue. You should peek inside. There's a whole article."

I suddenly felt sick and began to shake.

Looking around at everyone else, Angela gushed, "See, I told you she looked like her." Then she turned to me. "You're her.

You're Chloe-Grace Star, aren't you?!" Her hands were shaking with excitement.

I was speechless as I continued to read the article.

Pointing at Jack, Angela continued. "You're in it too."

I flushed and immediately dropped the magazine on the table and covered my face, feeling tears about to come pouring out. This was all too much. Without saying anything, I got up and rushed out of the lunchroom, too afraid to talk. As I made my way through the cafeteria, I heard all four of them yell, "Lilly! Wait!"

Without stopping, I headed straight for the girls' room, the only place I could think of to hide. A few seconds after I got inside, they all followed me in, including Jack.

Two girls already in the bathroom immediately screamed at him to get out. Undaunted, he ignored them. "Lilly, what's going on?"

I was holed up in a stall and had the door locked. I felt totally and utterly alone. Everyone was talking a mile a minute, with Angela's high-pitched voice carrying over everyone else's. "That means this is true, right? This is one hundred percent true? This is so crazy! I can't believe we have a celebrity in our school!"

Voices I didn't recognize joined in the chatter, all in confused and unbelieving excitement. "That's Chloe-Grace Star in there?"

I heard pages being flipped open. I wondered if I could conceivably flush myself down the toilet.

Jana peeked under the stall door. "Lilly. Chloe-Grace. Lilly. Just come out, please. I don't care what's going on. I just want to make sure you're okay."

"Ohmigod, I can't believe this is happening."

Jack's face appeared over the stall wall. "Lilly, this probably isn't even true. Angela's just jumping to conclusions. Aren't you, Angela?"

"I don't think so."

He turned to glare at her.

"Seriously, it's her. She's like, undercover, or something," she said with conviction. "The magazine can't be *that* wrong."

Reaching his arm under the door, Jack unlatched the lock and I didn't stop him. The door slowly swung open.

Angela, Stefanie, and the two other girls stood there staring at me while Jana got up and then took my hand, leading me out of the stall. One of the girls I didn't know asked, "So *are* you Chloe-Grace?"

Looking around at everyone's expectant faces, I couldn't deny it any longer. "Yes. I'm Chloe-Grace," I admitted. I turned around to glance at Jack. "I'm so sorry."

Angela exploded in delighted triumph. "I *so* knew it!"

I didn't even feel mad at her. I could understand why she was so exuberantly happy. This would be the biggest story of the year. For Angela, this was possibly the most exciting thing she'd had happen in her life.

"Angela, can I see the magazine?" I couldn't bear to think about what else the article said. Did they know about Henry? I had to know what the press knew. Turning over the magazine to me, everyone stayed silent while I slowly read it.

It basically said what Angela had blurted out. Chloe-Grace

Star, daughter of Dominique Benjamin and John Michael Star, had been enrolled at Hollis High for three weeks, living undercover as a noncelebrity. They also identified Luther as my caretaker. Worst of all, in a separate sidebar were pictures of me and Jack from our beach date. "Who's Chloe's new boy toy?" The way they made it sound, it was as if Jack was someone I had duped into dating me. The word *ensnared* leaped off the page.

I slumped against a wall and let the magazine drop to the ground. My mind flashed back to the creepy guy from the bookstore. "I can't believe this is happening," I mumbled wearily.

Still letting her imagination run wild, Angela asked, "Wait, are you doing some sort of reality show or something? Ohmigod, are there cameras around? Are we on some sort of social experiment?" Inexplicably, she started looking around the bathroom, as if she was expecting something.

"No. It's not a reality show." I sighed.

"So, what's going on?" Jana asked, genuinely concerned.

I looked up at her and then at Jack, who looked both sad and confused.

"I was just trying to get away for a while. Nobody really knows I'm here." Well, everybody would know now. Temporarily out of tears, I tried to compose myself. "I'm so sorry, guys. I didn't want it to be like this."

The girl who had asked if I really was Chloe-Grace reached into her purse and pulled out her camera-phone. "Can I take a picture with you?"

I covered my face with my hands and started crying again.

"Out. Out. Get out of here." Quickly taking matters into his own hands, Jack moved to usher the two girls out of the bathroom. They complained that he was the one who wasn't supposed to be in there, but he continued to push them out the door.

"Wait, please don't tell anybody!" I futilely called after them. Oh, what was the use? They couldn't possibly do more damage at this point.

"Guys, I have to get home. I can't stay here."

"I'll take you home," Jack offered immediately.

"Ooh, can I come? I'd love to see where a celebrity lives," Angela chimed in.

"Um, I don't think that's a great idea," Jana said, looking with concern at me. "Let's let Jack take her home."

I silently thanked her. I couldn't handle Angela's overenthusiasm right now. I felt as if my head was about to explode.

"Jana, can you come with us?" I wanted her along, partly because she'd already proved to be so caring and calm, partly because I wanted to explain things to her. Our friendship had already become important to me, and I knew she must have a million questions, even as she was managing the situation.

"Of course. Anything you want, Lilly."

Shaking my head, I said, "You guys can call me Chloe. There's no use pretending anymore."

As the five of us emerged from the bathroom, the hallways were littered with the usual lunchtime crowd, and people didn't seem to be overly excited. Thank goodness. I guess Angela had been the only one who'd seen the magazine so early. Jack, Jana, and I quickly ducked out and made our way into the parking lot toward his truck.

"This is totally unfair. I should get to come too," Angela said, trailing behind us.

I almost relented, but Jack put a stop to her whining by saying, "Look, my truck can barely fit the three of us as it is. I'm sure Lilly will be back to explain everything."

I nodded in assurance. Yeah, I would back. Followed by two million cameras and a news crew. Casting one last glance at Hollis as we took off, I wondered if there was any way I'd ever be allowed back at all. This was going to be it, the end of Lilly, the person I'd most wanted to be.

Riding home squeezed shoulder to shoulder in the cabin of the truck, Jack and Jana waited for me to say something.

I took a deep breath. "I'm so sorry for everything. I really thought I could do this. And it was working . . ." I trailed off.

"You don't have anything to apologize for, seriously. We're just confused," Jana said.

Sighing, I gave them as much of the story as I could. "So, I'm really Chloe-Grace Star. And I transferred from Newton because it'd been too crazy there with my parents getting divorced and the paparazzi everywhere."

As I talked, I kept inspecting Jack's face to see what he thought. He'd gotten awfully quiet and wasn't responding or asking very many questions. Jana, however, was really supportive, and although she didn't understand the magnitude of who my parents were, she understood that I'd been too famous to go to school comfortably.

By the time we arrived at Luther's house, I had told them everything—except about Henry. As we drove down Luther's street I saw a few random cars, and I knew that the cameras would come out soon.

We walked in amid Luther pinning a dress on a mannequin. Surprised to see the three of us enter, he immediately stopped what he was doing.

"Lilly, honey, what're you doing here?" He walked toward us to introduce himself. "How do you do? I'm Lilly's father, Luther."

Jack and Jana eyed him curiously and didn't respond. I shrugged. "Luther, it's over. Everyone knows I'm really Chloe-Grace. It was in a magazine this morning."

Luther clapped both hands to his mouth, and his eyes widened into saucers.

I sat, defeated, on the couch while Jack and Jana sat down on chairs across from me. My head was spinning, and emotional exhaustion was setting in.

"Okay. Okay. Umm, what should we do?"

"Call Mom, I guess?" I wasn't sure why the paparazzi hadn't popped their creepy little heads into the picture full force yet, but I knew it wouldn't be long before my mom found out I'd been exposed. "I guess people will be looking for me soon."

Jack stood up. "Um, maybe we should go now?"

Rising too quickly to my feet, I sat back down immediately

when everything got momentarily fuzzy. Everyone rushed over to me as I clutched my head. "No, don't go yet. I want you guys to stick around. I'm not sure when I'm going to see you again."

"You kids sit here. I'm going to go call Chloe's mom," Luther said, leaving the room.

"You're not coming back?" Jana asked.

I hesitated, even though I thought I knew the answer. "I'm not sure. Once everyone knows about this, I can't possibly go back. It's over, I guess." Saying it out loud to them—saying it out loud to myself—made it seem so much more final.

"Does that mean we won't see you again?"

My gut reaction was to say emphatically "Of course you will!" But I knew that everything was already entirely different, especially with Jack. "I'm not sure exactly. It's all just very sudden." Not pushing the matter any further, Jana excused herself to go to the bathroom.

Sitting alone, I looked over at Jack. I sensed that he was reeling, and his initial guardian instinct had now been overridden by confusion. "Jack? What are you thinking?" I reached over to touch his hand.

His eyes directed away from me and slowly panned over Luther's living room. He took a moment to reply. "I don't know. I'm thinking that I'm not sure who you are exactly. Did you come to Hollis to escape or to pretend? I guess I'm just confused about everything." He paused, then quietly added, "I wish you would have trusted me enough to tell me earlier. I mean, what does this mean for us? For our relationship?"

"Jack, my other life, it's really complicated. With you everything was just so easy. I feel exactly the same way about you as Lilly or as Chloe. I—"

Luther interrupted us by coming back into the room. "Your mom wants to talk to you." He handed me the phone, and I grabbed it and walked into the other room.

"Mom! I'm so sorry. I don't know how this happened."

"Okay, honey, we'll fix this. What happened?"

Hearing my mom's familiar voice brought back tears all over again. I struggled through the story of how Angela had shown me the magazine and how I'd escaped from Hollis.

"I don't know what to do anymore." That statement felt more true than ever. I really didn't know where I could go or what my life would be like. I couldn't possibly hide anymore, and the hope I'd held that I could escape from celebrity life was dealt a mortal blow.

"Chloe, it's fine. I already told Luther what to do. You're going to come to Capri. Right now. I can't leave the set, but we need to be together through this. The press will be all over the story, and I'm not going to not have you by my side when everything hits the fan. I'm going to send a plane for you. Just have Luther drive you to the airport and come over. We'll settle everything out here. Okay?"

Before getting off the phone, she sighed. "I guess we're going to have to tell your father too. I'll call him."

"Okay, bye, Mom. I'll see you soon. I love you."

I walked out into the main room, and Jack and Jana were

standing by the door. "My mom said I'm going to meet her in Capri. She's there shooting a movie and can't leave." I felt as if everything was still unresolved with Jack, but we didn't have time to sit down for a real talk.

"Okay, you have to go pack. Jack, Jana, I'm sorry, but you're going to have to leave," Luther said.

Both Jack and Jana gave me hugs.

"I'll call you guys as soon as I can."

As they walked out, Jack turned back to me, and I mouthed, "I'm sorry." He looked away and left.

I suddenly felt crazy overwhelmed. There were just so many loose ends all over the place. I had to let Vickie know what had happened. I had to let Rachelle know the whole story. Henry was still probably sitting in geometry class, wondering where I was. I contemplated sending a mass text to everyone, but that wouldn't do at all.

Not wanting to leave the country without talking to at least Vickie, I looked at the time. It was her free period, so I knew she'd pick up. I gave her a call as Luther drove us to the airport.

"Vick, it's all over. They found out I was at Hollis."

*"Ohmigod, what happened?"*

I rushed the explanation, because I didn't have time for much more.

"So, what can I do for you?"

"Nothing, I just wanted to let you know before anyone else because you've been in this thing since the beginning. I'm going to call Rach right now, but I'm not sure how much time I'll have to talk to her. If she wants, I'm going to have her call you for the full story, if that's okay. Otherwise, I'll fill her in when I get to Capri."

"No problem. Keep me updated on what happens. I'm here for you."

I smiled as I hung up and dialed Rachelle.

Rachelle, predictably for the middle of the day, didn't answer her phone. I sent her a text that said simply: "There's been a lot going on. I'll be away from the phone for a while. Talk to Vickie if you want to know right now. I'm so sorry. Miss you."

A few hours later we were in the air and on our way to Capri. Luther had transformed both of us for a quick getaway, and we'd avoided any media attention driving to a private airport near Long Beach, where we took a chartered plane. Taking off the long wig of hair I'd been wearing, I looked at my reflection in the airplane window. Lilly's face stared back, but I felt completely severed from her. I was back to being Chloe-Grace.

Since Capri is a small island with no way of directly flying in, we landed in Naples and from there took a car to the ferry dock. For the first time it occurred to me that this was a film that Luther wasn't working on with my mom. When I asked him why, he said, "You needed somebody to look after you, and I wasn't ready to go work on some beautiful tropical island for a few weeks. L.A. is so much smoggier this time of year." He gave me a dazzling smile.

It dawned on me that Luther had passed up the opportunity to work with my mom in order to open his house to me, to allow me to be Lilly.

"Oh, Luther. You're the best!" Reaching over to give him a hug, I thought about how much all my friends had been willing to help me even if they didn't understand everything I was going through exactly.

"Plus, this little indie film couldn't afford me anyway," Luther joked.

When we got out of the car, my mom was waiting for us and shockingly, standing beside her was my dad. I ran up to give them big hugs. They embraced me together, and for the briefest of moments it felt as if nothing had changed at all. When we pulled away, I took a hard look at my dad, dressed in blousy linen pants and a dress shirt only halfway buttoned. "What are you doing here?"

I looked back and forth between the two of them, waiting for an answer. My mom, with her long hair tied back high on her head and blowing in the wind, waited for him to explain. "When your mom called to tell me what had happened, I flew out here immediately. I was already in London, so I got here last night."

"And you're not mad?" I sounded incredulous.

"Well, your mother and I had some choice words for each other, but we're alright now; isn't that right, Dom?" They smiled at each other as if the past few weeks of media bickering and fighting had just been a bad dream. Maybe being on a beautiful Mediterranean island with a crisis that was my doing had been just what the doctor ordered.

The four of us strode up the ramp and onto the ferry. I had

expected my mom to be in conniptions, but it seemed as if she was perfectly relaxed and not at all worried about anything. My dad seemed to be really at ease too. As the ferry took us over to Capri, I leaned in to Luther and said, "What is going on here?" I pointed to my parents.

"Maybe the ocean air?" He was just as confused as I was.

Marveling at how nonchalant and unhurried the atmosphere among us was, I took the time to take in the bright blue ocean and try to relax. I didn't feel rushed to have to explain everything.

It wasn't until we were all fully settled on the garden patio at my mom's rental villa that my parents even asked me to detail what had been going on, which I tried my best to do, with a little help from Luther.

When I got to the part about how frustrating the divorce stuff had been, I noticed that my parents were constantly flashing meaningful looks at each other, as if they had something to talk about or they were sharing some secret conversation. "And so that's why I had to transfer." I took a deep breath and stopped talking.

"How long were you planning to transfer for?" my dad asked.

"I'm not really sure," I replied truthfully. "However long I could, I guess. I just didn't think it would be so quick that everything ended."

"Does this mean that you're going back to Newton now?" That was the question I'd been thinking about ever since we'd left Luther's. It didn't seem possible that I'd stay at Hollis. I mean, that wasn't my real life. How could I possibly stay there after everything that had happened? The only reasonable choice seemed to be to return to Newton.

There was a long silence as I tried to compose an answer. "I offered to take her out of school and just get her tutored if she wanted to," my mom explained. She turned to me. "You can still do that. Nobody would make you go to school if it's so horrible."

"No, it's not that I don't like school," I said, thinking of how much I'd actually miss interacting with my friends on a daily basis. "Hollis was actually really great for me. And Newton was sometimes too."

"So it's not really about going or not going to school. It's about how unhappy you are with your life. With your life with us." When she said this, I thought about how I hadn't even told them about my birth parents yet. I looked at Luther, who cleared his throat and gave me a meaningful look. I had to bring it up now.

"I've just been unhappy with me." I sighed. "I need to tell you something else, sort of related to all of this." I paused, and my parents waited for me to go on.

Taking a really deep breath, I steadied myself. "Part of the reason why I transferred was because I found my birth parents. They live in Alhambra, and my little brother actually goes to Hollis. That's how I chose that particular high school. So transferring was sort of a two-part issue for me." I waited nervously for their reaction.

My mom looked disappointed and hurt. "Chloe, you lied to me?"

"I didn't, not really. It was just something I wasn't ready to tell you yet. Both of you," I said, looking significantly at my dad. "I found them and decided that I'd like to get to know my brother a little bit but without any of the hoopla that would have come from being your daughter. I wanted to see them on my own terms."

"How do you know there would have been hoopla? You don't know what we would have done if you had just told us from the beginning."

I looked at her a bit accusingly. "There's always so much attention about anything you guys do. It's unavoidable."

Shaking his head, my dad said, "You've certainly been a busy girl."

"Did you know about this?" my mom asked Luther pointedly.

Not wanting her to be mad at him, I quickly cut in. "I just told him recently and made him swear not to tell you. Honestly, he didn't know anything about this before."

My parents looked at each other. "So, how are they?" my mom asked hesitantly.

"I don't know. I haven't gotten to know them yet. Just my brother. And he doesn't know who I am either. He just thinks I'm a friend in his class." Though not for long. This would ruin everything. Aside from possibly alienating everyone at Hollis, the thought of the friendship with Henry ending so abruptly seemed incredibly unfair. I felt as if this made it that much harder to tell him I was his sister. I had to make sure he still even wanted to be friends first. There was no way I could drop two bombshells on him at the same time.

"Well, this is going to take a while to digest. But in the meantime, we need to figure out what to do. I'll call David and see if he can tone down the tabloids. I have another two weeks left here on the shoot, and I was hoping that you'd want to stay until we can go back together," my mom offered.

"What about school?"

"Let's worry about that when we get to it. You're in no place right now to go back, anyway. John, I think you should stay too."

My dad didn't look all that surprised, although both Luther and I were.

"I agree. It sounds like we really need some family time together."

"Chloe, why don't you get unpacked while your father and I talk."

I nodded and made my way upstairs to my bedroom. After winding down, I decided it was time to call Rachelle and tell her what was going on.

"Chloe-Grace!" she screamed, picking up the phone after one ring. "You are absolutely insane. I can't believe you did this." I held the phone away from my ear as she continued. "Absolutely stunning. You've been having a whole bunch of fun without me!"

I had been really worried that Rachelle would be upset that I hadn't told her, but it turned out that she was only mad that I hadn't asked her to join me in disguising ourselves. I sighed. That was Rachelle for you.

"What, did you think I couldn't do it? Transfer schools and go anonymous? I totally could have, you know. Then we could have both been revealed together." Even though everything had changed, it felt good that Rachelle was still the same.

"So, are you really in Capri now? The press has no idea where you went off to." She laughed as if it was the most amusing thing ever.

"Yes, I'm really in Capri now."

"And there's obviously no hot production assistant, right? It's this guy they showed in the magazine?" How like Rachelle to get right to the heart of the matter.

"Yeah, he's this guy from school. And I guess we were sort of dating, maybe. I have no idea now."

I thought about Jack and how we had left things. I really missed him. I hoped the media weren't hounding him.

"Oh please, I'm sure you'll still be together. He's dating a celeb!" Rachelle said. Exactly, and I wasn't sure Jack wanted to be involved in that whole scene.

"So when am I going to see you? You totally have to tell me everything."

"Well, I'm here in Capri for at least two weeks, then I'll be home."

"And when are you coming back to Newton?"

I paused. "I don't know. Things are really up in the air right now."

"Okay, stop keeping me out of the loop and tell me as soon as you figure it out. I cannot wait for you to come home. It's going to be so crazy! Miss you!"

I hung up, after telling her I missed her too. I was a bit relieved though. The longer I talked to Rachelle, the more unwilling I was to go back to my old life.

Later that night my mom and dad approached me as I sat on the patio, overlooking the ocean.

"How are you doing, sweetie?" my mom asked.

I sighed. "Fine. Just thinking about everything that's happened the past few weeks."

My parents nodded.

"So, Chloe, we're going to hold a press conference tomorrow to clear up what's been going on. You don't have to go, of course, but it would be nice if you were there. Your dad and I will do all the talking. The three of us being there together would go a long way toward showing everyone that we're still a family," my mom said.

"But that's not really true. We aren't still a family," I replied.

My parents looked at each other. "We understand that part of what drove you to do this was how estranged you'd been feeling from us. Your mother and I talked, and we've decided to put the divorce on hold while trying to figure out how to make the situation right again. Or at least workable."

"You guys aren't going to get divorced?" I was afraid it sounded too good to be true.

Looking significantly at each other before answering, my mom then said, "Well, I'm not so sure about that. But we're willing to not be rash and to see what we can work out. Our main concern is you, something we might have forgotten recently. We'll try to work it out internally this time instead of fight each other in the press."

That was a start, I guess. Even if my parents weren't completely committed to not divorcing, at least they would give it some thought. I felt as if we could finally talk again.

"I think I can come tomorrow. If that's what you guys want."

"You'd be comfortable doing that?"

"Yeah, I would." And I was. Having seen how grown-up and forgiving my parents were acting, toward me and each other, I thought it could only be a good thing if we all approached everything with a fresh start.

After they said their good nights and both gave me a kiss, I was alone again. I thought about the past three weeks. How much I liked being Lilly and having a normal life. How I really wanted to find my birth parents. How I liked my new friends, and Jack. But I also realized that I missed my adoptive parents too. That while I liked Lilly's life, I was still Chloe-Grace. And nothing was going to change that.

But maybe now I could be Chloe-Grace on my own terms.


The next morning I woke up and walked downstairs to see David standing in the middle of the villa courtyard. He was way overdressed as usual, this time in a full-on dark suit and tie.

"What're you doing here?" I asked.

"Taking care of the press conference," he replied, very businesslike. "The reporters are going to ask you questions anyway, even though I told them you wouldn't be answering. When they do, just don't answer, and I'll take care of everything. Got it?"

Yawning, I said, "Sure thing." Man, even in another country David was uptight.

Half an hour later, my parents and I took a ferry to a hotel conference room. Reporters were jammed in the room, and I was feeling a mild sense of panic just seeing them. Murmurs turned to a noisy din as soon as we entered.

Once we were settled at the front of the room behind a long table, David raised a hand to silence the crowd. Amazingly, they all stopped talking.

"We'll be taking one question at a time, but first Dominique would like to say something. Please hold your questions until she's finished."

My mom stood up and spoke firmly into the mike as camera flashes went off in the audience. In her clear voice, so familiar to millions of people, she began. "As you know, we've been having a little family drama lately. But John and I are happy to announce that we're no longer pursuing a divorce. We've decided to try and work things out."

A sea of hands flung into the air as everyone began to blurt out questions. My mom raised her hand to hush the crowd and continued. "We both realize, perhaps a bit belatedly, that family is the most important thing in both of our lives. And we just want to stand together, with Chloe, and make everything right again. Thank you."

A barrage of voices created a cacophony throughout the room. But all I kept hearing was my name. "Did Chloe ... Is Chloe ... When will Chloe ... Chloe! Chloe!"

David stood up. "People, please. We can't take more than one question at once!"

After a few minutes of chaos, the din finally settled down. One reporter's question rang out above everything else: "Chloe, did you know your parents were filing for divorce?"

My mom looked quickly over at me. "No, Chloe did not know we were filing for divorce," she answered. "And in fact, we hadn't fully decided on what we were going to do yet when she found out."

"Chloe, were you trying to escape your parents when you transferred to Hollis?

"Please, we'd rather not have any questions directed to Chloe," my dad replied. "She's here to support us and not to answer any questions."

The reporters ignored him and filled the air with another round of Chloe-related questions. "Is Chloe going to be returning to Newton?"

Seeing my parents trying to deflect attention away from me, trying to answer questions that only I could truthfully answer, I realized that I needed to speak up for myself.

I flicked on the microphone in front of me. "Actually, Dad, I don't mind. Really, it's okay."

Both of my parents looked at me, surprised. David looked alarmed that I'd disregarded his directions.

I took a deep breath and faced the crowd. This was my life they were questioning. I needed to respond on my terms. Feeling more confident than ever, I said, "I most certainly didn't decide to transfer schools because of my parents. I was just curious about what life was like as a normal teen, that's all." I decided to leave out the part about my biological parents. I gave the assembled crowd the biggest smile I could muster. "And I'm not sure when— or if—I'll be going back to Newton."

I looked at my parents and smiled, then turned back to the reporters. "That's all I'm going to say right now."

Both of them look back at me and smiled, and then turned to the assembled reporters.

"I think we're about done here, now," my mom said. Her smile was gentle and encouraging.

After the press conference Luther rushed up to give me a hug. "I'm so proud of you!"

I was proud of myself too. I hadn't been nervous or scared, or felt intruded upon. I'd been surprised at how comfortable I felt talking to the media. I'd never tried that before, but it had felt right. I realized that if I was to come to terms with my life, celebrity or not, I would have to take ownership of my decisions. I resolved not to let the actions of other people, especially total strangers, completely color everything I did. I felt relieved.

# Chapter
## 13

While my mom was finishing her movie, my dad and I took time for some old-fashioned father-daughter bonding. But I also kept some time for myself to think more about things.

I had e-mailed Jana to talk with her about everything—explain things to her. She, like Vickie, was understanding and a true friend. I also talked to Vickie and gave her more details about everything that had happened. She updated me on the goings-on at Newton, about Austin and Stacey, and Rachelle.

But the one person I was most concerned about—the one person I hadn't heard from—was Jack. Despite the three e-mails I'd sent and the two phone messages I'd left, I hadn't gotten a response.

And then there was Henry. I still didn't know what I was going to say to him, how I was going to tell him I'm actually his sister. And I hadn't really figured out how I was going to meet my birth parents.

I suddenly felt an urgency to get back to the States. It dawned on me that I couldn't just stay here; there were relationships to repair back home.

Once again I turned to Luther for help.

"So, Luther, I think I need to go back to L.A., like, today."

Luther looked up at me from poolside and sighed. "This wouldn't have anything to do with Jack and Henry, would it?"

I smiled. "Umm, maybe? Please, Luther. I've been doing a lot of thinking this week, and I don't think I can be here another whole week while my life hangs in the balance at home."

"Don't we think we're being a little dramatic?"

"No. Well, maybe. But I really need to do this. I need to make things right with Jack. And I need to tell Henry the truth."

Luther lifted his sunglasses and stared at me. "Fine, I'll talk to your mom. Besides, Capri was starting to bore me a little."

"Really?"

"No, honey. It's Capri! But anything for you."

"Thanks, Luther." I beamed.

So after five days in Capri, I was headed home with Luther. I asked my dad if he wanted to go, but he said that he and my mom still had some things to work out. They had been talking a lot, and I crossed my fingers that they were really ready to try again.

When we arrived at Luther's on Thursday night, I immediately called Vickie.

"You were amazing!"

"What are you talking about?" I asked, a bit confused.

"Your standout performance at the press conference! I saw it online, and you looked so great and confident and self-assured. It was brilliant!"

"Thanks. That means a lot to me."

"So, what are your plans now that you're back?"

"Well, first things first, I need to talk to Jack. And then I have to find Henry and explain everything."

"You just have to be honest with everyone, especially Jack. You guys were so good together before all of this. I'm sure he remembers that."

"I know."

"Just be the person you have always been, regardless of whether you were called Chloe or Lilly. You are who you are, and Jack—and Henry—will understand that."

I sighed. Vickie was right. I am the same person. I just had to convince Jack and Henry of that.

"Thanks, Vickie! It's really good to be home again."

I called Jack as soon as I hung up with Vickie, and he answered after one ring. After a short awkward chat, I asked him to come over. Reluctantly, he agreed. Even though it was late and I was tired from jet lag, I needed to see him in person and explain everything.

As his truck pulled up outside the house thirty minutes later, I went out to meet him.

"Hey. I'm sorry I left without explaining everything," I started, climbing into the passenger seat.

Jack nodded. "It's okay. You didn't have time. I understand," he said quietly.

"You were amazing that day, seriously. I wanted to thank you."
He nodded again, but it was hard to tell how he was feeling.

"So, I think I owe you an explanation." And after pausing,
I told him everything, from the divorce, to wanting to change
schools, even to my birth parents and Henry. When I was finished,
we sat in uncomfortable silence for a while. I fought the urge to
just shake him into talking. Finally, he leaned back into his seat
and exhaled deeply.

"I'm worried that what we had the last couple of weeks at
school was just a lie. I'm not really sure exactly who you are. I
mean, you're Chloe-Grace Star. You're famous."

"That doesn't matter to me. Does it to you?"

"Well, does anything change now that you're not Lilly?" He
had turned his head to look directly at me.

"Not if you don't want it to."

Even as I said this, I knew that wasn't exactly true. Everything
would change. I couldn't have a relationship without it being
heavily scrutinized. And Jack would now have to deal with the
paparazzi and tabloids. That would change things a lot. But it
didn't change how I felt about him. Not one bit.

"Do you think it changes anything?" I asked. "I feel the same
way about you as Chloe or Lilly; it doesn't matter."

"So you don't care that I'm a nobody?"

"Does my being famous mean that I'm somebody?"

Taking a moment to respond, he smiled. "Well, it certainly
makes me worried about how many hot guys must be in love
with you."

"There's only one hot guy I'm in love with." I laughed, and leaned in and gave him a kiss. "And that's you, if you think you can handle it."

"Well, I guess that sounds okay . . . Chloe." He tilted my chin up with his hand and kissed me again.

We sat silently for a few minutes before we continued talking. Jack had a lot of questions about the tabloids and cameras, and I tried to explain the insanity as best I could. Having reassured him that while things may change, our relationship could stay exactly the same, we vowed not to let the paparazzi interfere as best we could and just continue as if we were two regular people.

With another kiss good night, I went inside. I was exhausted, and tomorrow was going to be another big day. I was ready to talk to Henry and explain everything. And I was ready meet my birth parents now. I didn't want to wait for the perfect opportunity. I didn't want to wait for anything anymore.

Henry was still groggy when I called him at six o'clock and woke him up. I asked if he wouldn't mind meeting me outside. I hadn't slept nearly the whole night and had waited patiently until it was a somewhat decent hour to head over to his house.

Still sleepy, he came outside and got into the car. "Hey, Lilly, um, Chloe. What're you doing here?"

"So you've heard, huh."

"I may not be popular in school, but I do watch TV. Why didn't you tell me?"

"Oh, Henry." I sighed. I had thought long and hard about

what I wanted to say. I had a whole speech prepared, but looking at him, I couldn't remember it anymore. I forged ahead anyway. "Listen, I need to talk to you about something. More than just about who I was. Or wasn't."

He sat up at attention in the seat, rubbing the drowsiness out of his eyes. "What do you mean?"

Taking a deep breath, I poured out, "I'm adopted. My real parents are from China, and my adoptive parents, John and Dominique, adopted me from there when I was a baby. So part of me transferring to Hollis was to find my birth parents. And the reason I chose Hollis is because . . . I found out that we're related."

I let that sink in for a moment, but Henry looked confused. I continued. "I found out that your parents, our parents, were the ones who put me up for adoption. You're my brother, Henry. And that's why I decided to transfer to Hollis in the first place. To meet you."

Fully awake now, Henry was startled. "Are you kidding me?"

I shook my head. "I'm totally serious."

"Are you sure?"

"Positive. I got information from the adoption agency. I can prove everything to you if you want." I had brought the entire file of paperwork that Jean-Paul had given me. The folder was sitting in my backseat.

Realizing that I was one hundred percent genuine, he pulled his head up and let out a long sigh. "You don't need to prove it. I believe you. Even if you weren't my real sister, I'd want you to be anyway."

I sucked in a breath. All this time I was friendly with Henry, I never stopped to think about how he felt about our friendship. That one statement summed up everything. I started to tear up and couldn't hold back my emotions any longer. Seeing me start to cry, Henry reached out and gave me an awkward hug.

"Chloe, maybe you should come inside. Don't you think?"

Reaching for a tissue, I wiped my tears. "Yeah, I think so," I whispered.

As we walked down the path to his condo, I reached out for his hand and he took it, albeit a bit uncomfortably. I started to feel more waterworks well up inside me, and as we reached the door, I got really scared.

"Henry, did your parents ever mention to you that you had a sister?"

"No, never." That made me even more nervous, but it was too late. Henry had already opened the door and led me in. I walked in and immediately felt entirely out of place. The room was cramped and still dark from the shades being halfway drawn. I could hear clattering in the kitchen and then an older female voice, tinged with an accent, asking, "Hong-Yin, where did you go?"

Looking at me and squeezing my hand in reassurance, Henry said, "Mom, come out here."

When she emerged from the kitchen, I sucked in a breath. I was staring at my birth mother. She looked small, but I could see my eyes and cheekbones in her face. She was carrying a cup of tea; and when she saw me, she dropped it, sending the cup crashing to the floor.

As she started speaking in frantic Chinese, we both rushed over to make sure she was okay. She didn't take even one look at the mess on the ground and just grabbed my hands. "Shao-Chi! Shao-Chi!" Much to my happy surprise and astonishment, my birth mom knew exactly who I was.

My mom called to my father, who came running. He too recognized me and gave me a big hug. We all sat down—as a family—and talked for hours.

Apparently my birth parents had known who I was the whole time. They recognized me from all the baby pictures that had appeared in the magazines and connected it with the famous American celebrity parents who had adopted me. My mother cried as she told me about how hard it had been for them to give me away, but they had no choice because they couldn't have a daughter, only a son.

"We knew you were here, with famous parents. We knew you were safe and having a good life. We did not want to interfere," she said.

"Of course we wanted to contact you, but we could not. Your life seemed so wonderful and your parents, so beautiful. We knew you had the best life, that we could not offer," my father continued, his eyes rimmed with tears.

While I wanted to be angry and upset with this news—after all, if they knew about me, why wouldn't they want to find me—I understood their logic on some level. Why would they want to interfere in what appeared to everyone to be a perfect life.

As I struggled to contain my crying, I tried to tell them that even though my life was wonderful, I'd been thinking about them for a while and that I had been searching for them and needed to know who they were.

At a certain point, my mom went upstairs and returned with a large, oversize scrapbook into which she had stuffed numerous articles, pictures, and news clippings of me. Henry was astonished to see this book, and as we flipped through it, he kept rubbing his head in bewilderment.

I then explained to everyone how I had switched to Hollis High in order to befriend Henry—Hong-Yin—and they already knew about how much I'd been trying to help him and to look out for him. They said that I was already a true sister, and I felt relief at our meeting having gone so perfectly.

As I left their house, after two hours of talking and tearful laughing and promising to return soon, Henry walked with me back to the car.

"Is it okay if I call you *jie* now?"

"What does that mean?"

"It's 'older sister' in Chinese. I'd call you Lilly, I mean, Chloe in front of everyone else, though," he said.

Reaching over to hug him, I said, "You can call me whatever you want. As long as I can do this!" And I gave him a little punch on the arm and then mussed his new hairdo.

He punched me right back, just like a brother ought to do.

As I drove back to Luther's, I was completely overwhelmed by everything that had just happened. I had found my birth family! And I had the answers to questions that had been bugging me for so long. Sitting there with me, in their own home, was the part of me that had been missing. I felt complete, and ready to face the world. Finally.

And there was no way the paparazzi would get hold of this story until I was good and ready. My biological parents certainly wouldn't tell anyone, Henry was sworn to silence by his older sister, and everyone else could be trusted to stay quiet, even Rachelle (if I begged her to). I wasn't trying to be secretive or anything. I just needed everything to come out on my own terms. I wanted to take control of my life.

I know, that's nothing particularly special. Just totally, awesomely normal.

# Epilogue

Three months later . . .

Jack and I walked hand in hand into Great Eats Market. I'd gotten him addicted to gummy penguins. It's number two on our list of favorite things to do together. Number one on that list is, of course, singing together, karaoke style, even if my off-pitch renditions make him cringe now and again. You know someone truly loves you if he's willing to put up with, even encourage, you ruining his eardrums.

Moving toward the back of the store, I broke into a little skip and dragged him along.

"Hurry up, slowpoke!" Looking at me like I was crazy, he shook his head and caught up to me. We attracted a few sideways glances as we made our way down the aisles, but neither of us cared if anyone looked at us.

I grabbed a gummy penguin from the bin and popped it into Jack's mouth, and followed it up immediately with a big kiss.

"Ummm, I'll take another one of those," he said as I pulled away.

"How about a lot of those?" I held up two empty plastic bags and raised my eyebrows teasingly. He answered by picking up the candy shovel and dropping a huge scoop into one of the bags.

A few minutes later we strolled up to the checkout counter. Glancing over the magazine rack while waiting behind a few other customers, I saw an inset picture of me on the cover of *Starfan*. I have to admit, the picture actually looked kind of okay. A mini-headline read "Chloe-Grace Revealed!"

Smiling at Jack, I handed him my bag of gummies and picked up a copy of the magazine. Quickly flipping it open to my article on page twenty-one, the first sentence I read was: "Chloe-Grace Star and her beautiful boy toy, Jack, are headed for a difficult crosstown romance, as she's chosen to return to Newton while he remains at the high school he shared with her anonymous alter ego, Lilly. Can their already rocky relationship last?"

Seriously? I rolled my eyes and stopped reading. I wasn't even going back to Newton. Get one fact right at least, jeez.

I had decided to stay at Hollis because I wanted to finish out the year with my new friends. I wanted them to get to know the real me, and transferring back could always wait until next year. Plus, there was that beautiful "boy toy" of mine to hang out with.

Showing him the article, I said, "Look, you're famous again." Jack read the paragraph and laughed.

"I didn't realize our relationship was so rocky," he said with mock sincerity.

"Oh, it certainly is! Anything you read in here is absolutely one hundred percent true." I cocked an eyebrow at him. "So, what are you going to do about it?"

Pausing for just a second, Jack swept me up in his arms and began smothering me with kisses.

I was totally wrong. Gummy penguins and singing together should both be dropped down a notch on our list of favorite things to do. Kissing was definitely number one.